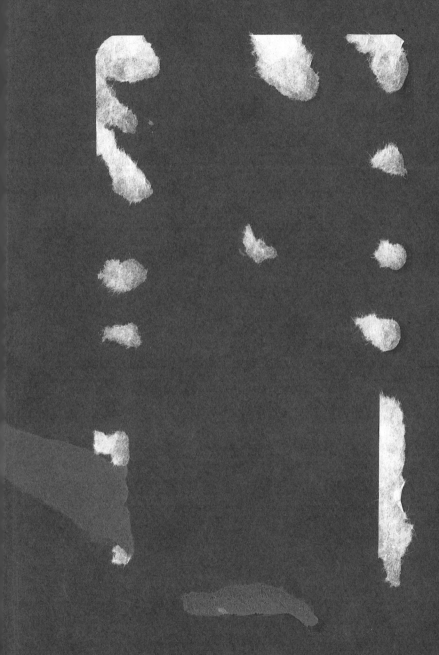

Living in a Risky World

Other Books by Laurence Pringle

Animals and Their Niches
The Earth Is Flat and Other Great Mistakes
Frost Hollows and Other Microclimates
Here Come the Killer Bees
The Minnow Family
Natural Fire
Vampire Bats

Living in a Risky World

Laurence Pringle

Morrow Junior Books / New York

TABLE CREDITS

Page 19: Adapted from Paul Slovic et al. "Facts and Fears: Understanding Perceived Risks."
In *Societal Risk Assessment: How Safe is Safe Enough?* edited by R. Schwing and
W. A. Albers, Jr., New York: Plenum Press, 1980.

Page 21: Adapted from Paul Slovic et al. In *Perilous Progress: Managing the Hazards of
Technology,* edited by Robert Kates et al. Boulder, Colorado: Westview Press, 1985.

Page 27: Adapted from Richard Wilson. "The Daily Risks of Life." *Technology Review,*
February 1979.

Page 28: Adapted from B. L. Cohen and I. S. Lee. "A Catalog of Risks." *Health Physics*
36, 1979.

PHOTO CREDITS

Permission for photographs is gratefully acknowledged: American Lung Association,
p. 38; Consumer Product Safety Commission, p. 78; Ecology and Environment, Inc., p. 5;
Food and Drug Administration, p. 40; *The Fresno Bee,* p. 15; General Public Utilities
Nuclear Corporation, p. 32; Insurance Institute for Highway Safety, p. 47; Jim Knight,
courtesy of Powell-Peralta Corporation, p. 9; Reproduced from the Collections of the
Library of Congress, pp. 3, 67; National Aeronautics and Space Administration, p. 11;
National Archives, p. 70; New York State Health Department, p. 86; Philadelphia Museum
of Art: Purchased: SmithKline Beckman Corporation Fund, p. 36; U.S. Dept. of
Agriculture, pp. 44, 57; U.S. Dept. of Agriculture, Forest Service, p. vi (Del Mar Jaquish).
All other photographs by the author.

Printed in the United States of America
1   2   3   4   5   6   7   8   9   10
Library of Congress Cataloging-in-Publication Data
Pringle, Laurence P.
Living in a risky world / Laurence Pringle.
p.   cm.
Bibliography: p.
Includes index.
Summary: Discusses the risks our society faces every day as we deal
with frightening uncertainties about food, transportation, clothing,
air, disease, natural disasters, and almost every area of our lives.
ISBN 0-688-04326-7.
1. Environmental health—Juvenile literature.   2. Health risk
assessment—Juvenile literature.   [1. Environmental health.
2. Health risk assessment.   3. Risk assessment.]   I. Title.
RA566.27.P75   1989
363—dc 19   88-31686   CIP   AC

Contents

Life Is Risky

The richest, longest-lived, best-protected, most resourceful civilization, with the highest degree of insight into its own technology, is on its way to becoming the most frightened. Has there ever been, one wonders, a society that produced more uncertainty more often about everyday life?
—*Aaron Wildavsky*, Risk and Culture

At the top of the ski slope, Lester Lave faces a choice. Safety or fun? He can loosen the screws of his ski bindings so they will release easily. This may spare him an injury but may also cut short an exciting run. Or he can tighten the screws so the bindings will release only under great force. This increases the chances of a long run—and of serious injury.

Twice he has made the wrong choice, taking spectacular falls that resulted in a broken shoulder and a cracked vertebra. "Every time, at the top of the hill, I make that choice," said Lave. "A quarter turn to the right or left."

Lester Lave may dwell on this choice a bit longer than most downhill skiers. That's because Lave, an economics professor at

Downhill skiers flirt with danger, risking injury in return for an exciting run and feelings of accomplishment.

Carnegie-Mellon University in Pittsburgh, was in 1986 president of the Society of Risk Analysis. But all skiers, and all people, make scores of choices every day about the hazards in life.

Richard Wilson of the Department of Physics and Environmental Policy at Harvard University once wrote a chronicle of some possible hazards he faced in a typical day:

> The moment I climb out of bed I start taking risks. As I drowsily turn on the light I feel a slight tingle: my house is old with old wiring and there is a small risk of electrocution. Every year 500 people are electrocuted in the United States. . . . I walk down to breakfast, taking care not to fall upon the stairs. Falls kill 16,000 people per year—mostly in domestic accidents. Shall I drink coffee or tea with my breakfast? Both contain caffeine, a well-known stimulant which may be carcinogenic. I have a sweet tooth; do I use sugar which makes me fat and gives me heart disease, or saccharin which we now know causes cancer?

As the morning went on, Wilson had to choose his mode of travel to and from work. By car, bicycle, or bus? There are dangers in each, but statistically the bus is safest. At work he was exposed to hazards involuntarily: tobacco smoke from colleagues at a meeting, radioactive radon gas from the bricks and cinder blocks of his office wall. At day's end he speculated about the danger of fire in bed and about a cancer-causing substance that was formerly used as a flame-retardant in pajamas.

Life has always been risky and always will be. We take hundreds of risks in our everyday lives, usually without much thought about them. In many ways, however, these are the safest, least hazardous times on earth, especially in the United States and other industrialized nations. For a dramatic comparison with the past, we need not look as far back as the devastating plagues of the Middle Ages. Just consider conditions at the beginning of this century, when more than 13 percent of American children died before their first birthday. The average life expectancy for adults was only about forty-eight years. Such diseases as diphtheria, tuberculosis, smallpox, cholera, and typhus were common and often fatal. Many medicines were unreliable; food and water were often contaminated. Laborers, including children, had little protection from the many hazards of their workplaces.

Today most of these threats to health are greatly reduced. We have almost conquered some of the most dangerous infectious diseases, as well as those caused by lack of vitamins and minerals. In industrialized Western countries, infant mortality rates are low and life expectancy grows longer. People now expect to live well into their seventies. More people are living longer, healthier lives.

Nevertheless, many people are deeply concerned about their health and safety. Many feel that recently life has become *more*

The "good old days" included diseases that are now uncommon and medicines that were ineffective or even harmful.

risky. According to a national opinion poll conducted in 1980, more than three out of four adult Americans believed that life was riskier than in 1960.

The 1960s, in general, saw a heightened risk consciousness in many Americans. In the years immediately following World War II, the public mood was confident and marked with great faith in technology. One success story of the time was the pesticide DDT, which had been dramatically effective in protecting Allied troops from typhus and other insect-transmitted diseases. At home it seemed to be a potent weapon against other insect pests.

Gradually, however, scientists discovered that DDT harmed not just pests but many other living things. They also detected DDT everywhere—in soils, plants, animals, air, water, foods, and even in human flesh. These discoveries were themselves a result of modern technology—use of new ways to measure chemical concentrations of just a few parts per million. The threat of DDT to living things, including humans, was brought to the attention of the public by Rachel Carson's powerful book, *Silent Spring,* and by the controversy the book aroused. Published in 1962, *Silent Spring* warned of the dangers of DDT and similar pesticides. It shook the blind faith that many people had in modern human inventions. The fruits of technology, it seemed, sometimes harbored worms.

In the early 1960s Americans also learned that automobiles were polluting the air they breathed. Unforeseen side effects from medicinal drugs and other products kept popping up. Trust in modern technology continued to erode, as did trust in manufacturers of products and government agencies that were supposedly regulating them. Ralph Nader's 1965 book, *Unsafe at Any Speed,* about safety defects in automobiles, contributed to a growing distrust of corporate America.

Some observers trace today's risk consciousness to the development of nuclear weapons. In 1945, most United States citizens approved of the use of atomic bombs at Hiroshima and Nagasaki

People today worry less about infectious diseases and more about toxic substances in foods, water, and the air.

as a means of quickly ending the war with Japan. By the early 1960s, the dangers of radiation had become better understood and more widely known. Like DDT, radioactivity from the explosion of nuclear weapons was recognized as a *global* problem. The Soviet Union developed its own nuclear arsenal, and a future war more horrifying than any in history loomed in people's imaginations.

Some threats, like nuclear weapons and cancer, have been worrying people for decades. Others reach a peak of attention and concern, then fade away. Every age has its list of major health and safety scares. Those of the 1970s include food dyes, saccharin, nitrates, pesticides, PCBs (polychlorinated biphenyls), and the sexually transmitted disease herpes. Those of the 1980s include AIDS (acquired immune deficiency syndrome), toxic wastes, radon, passive smoking, and excess salt and fat in diets.

Ironically, people worry more about their health and safety because modern technology, for all its benefits, gives them more to worry about. We know more about our environment, partly because chemists can now detect substances in parts per billion. Now they can identify potential health hazards that were previously undetected in the food, water, and air we take into our bodies. People used to worry about natural catastrophes, everyday accidents, infectious diseases, and acute poisons. Now they have broadened their concern to include technological troubles of global scale, chronic low-level hazards from chemicals, radiation, and a seemingly endless list of potential new health hazards.

At the same time that we have been learning more about hazards, we have grown to expect progress toward greater safety and good health. Twin revolutions have occurred—in science and technology, *and* in social expectations. According to William W. Lowrance, director of the Life Sciences and Public Policy Program at the Rockefeller University in New York, "In our knowing so much more and aspiring to so much more, we have passed beyond the sheltering blissfulness of ignorance and risk-enduring resignation."

William Lowrance wrote in 1983, "Now, about many hazards we know enough, scientifically, to 'worry,' but not enough to know *how much* to worry—or how much protective action to invest."

These questions are the heart of the matter, and of this book. The following chapters describe how people, including scientists and the general public, are struggling to answer them. *Living in a Risky World* does not cover in fine detail all of life's modern hazards—such information can go quickly out-of-date as a result of scientific discoveries, medical advances, or actions by government agencies. Rather, the book aims to give readers some insights that can be applied to all hazards, and suggestions for making life less risky.

CHAPTER 1

Perceptions of Risk

Thinking about uncertainty is very difficult for people—for experts as well as laypeople.
—Paul Slovic, Decision Research

John Elliot was a shy man, but on this evening he had come to a town meeting to speak his piece. There was a proposal for a new county garbage-burning plant to be built on some vacant land within half a mile of his home. Visibly nervous, John Elliot puffed on a cigarette as he waited for the meeting to start. When the time for public comments came, he rose from his seat. Speaking with a strained voice, he listed hazards of the proposed plant—increased traffic of heavy, smelly trucks, toxic metals in the plant's ashes, air pollutants including dioxin that might be emitted.

After the meeting, John Elliot felt hopeful that the county government would change its plans. The threat of the garbage-burning plant receded from his thoughts. He relaxed with a cigarette as he drove home.

The character and situation are fictitious, but there are scores of such issues, meetings, and protests in American communities each year. Thousands of citizens seek to keep landfills, power plants, and similar facilities from their neighborhoods. "Not in my backyard" is their cry. They focus on such hazards as radiation and pollutants that may get into the air, water, or soil. Paradox-

Cigarette smoking is a well-known health hazard that people begin voluntarily. Its addiction is then hard to break.

ically, some of the protestors smoke cigarettes. Also, as they drive to and from meetings where they fight for a less risky life, many of them fail to use their seat belts.

This doesn't make sense. The adverse health effects of smoking are widely known. Smoking is responsible for nine out of ten cases of lung cancer, a third of all heart disease deaths, and the vast majority of deaths from emphysema and chronic bronchitis. As for automobile accidents, they kill about 50,000 people each year in the United States. If every driver and passenger wore seat belts, more than half of these lives would be saved. Nevertheless, only about one out of seven drivers fastens his or her seat belt. Chances are many more citizens who protest against a garbage-burning plant will die in auto accidents or from a smoking-related illness than from pollutants emitted from such a facility.

Such paradoxes abound in human behavior. There is, however, a kind of crazy logic in the ways that people deal with the great diversity of risks in their lives. Thanks to studies conducted in the 1970s and early 1980s, we have a better understanding of how people perceive risk. Some of these studies, and their findings, are described in this and the following chapter.

Before looking at them, however, it is important to first note that risks and hazards are not the same thing. *Hazards* are threats to people and what they value. *Risks* are measures of the likelihood of harm or loss from hazards. The word *risk* implies both the existence of a threat and its potential for happening.

Control and Confidence

People have subtle and complex feelings about risks. Psychologists have made some discoveries about what people mean when they say something is or isn't risky and what factors underlie these perceptions.

A key factor, one that is involved in smoking and seat-belt use, is whether a hazard is voluntary. People are much more willing to

For fun, people voluntarily choose many risky activities.
They feel in control and able to minimize the risk.

take greater risks in activities or situations in which they feel they have some control than in activities or situations where they have little or no control. So people may smoke, drink, drive recklessly, or go hang gliding, feeling comfortable with the hazards—to the extent they understand them—because they feel in control. Involuntary hazards, such as pollutants from industry, additives in foods, and being passengers (not pilots) on commercial airlines, scare people more. They tend to feel powerless and more vulnerable to involuntary hazards.

The feeling of choosing our risks is comforting, but the amount of control we have over hazards may be illusory. Automobile drivers feel in control of their destiny, but even the best defensive driving techniques cannot prevent some accidents. For example, a person who chooses to go for a drive may become the involuntary victim of another driver who chooses to both drink and drive.

Overconfidence is another common—and dangerous—factor that humans apply to their judgments about risks. People tend to be overconfident about their ability to drive and to operate tools and other sometimes-hazardous devices safely. When people have direct control over their own safety, the thought "it won't happen to me" often gives unrealistic comfort. This characteristic has been revealed in many tests and is not an exclusive property of the general public. There are many cases of unwarranted confidence by engineers, scientists, and other experts.

Regarding the 1986 explosion of the space shuttle *Challenger,* a risk researcher said, "The way they were using the shuttle— sending up senators and schoolteachers—they were acting as though the risk of catastrophe might be as low as one in ten thousand, whereas the real risk might have been one in twenty, or one in fifty, or one in a hundred."

The tendency of people to overvalue their judgment was revealed in a study in which lottery tickets were sold to two groups of people in an office. Everyone paid a dollar apiece for the tickets,

Overconfidence about the safety of the space shuttle *Challenger* led to its explosion just after launching in early 1986.

but the individuals in one group were simply handed their tickets while those in the second group actually chose theirs. Then, just before the lottery drawing, the people were asked whether they would resell their tickets. Those who had simply been handed tickets were willing to sell them for an average price of $1.96. Those who had chosen their tickets asked for an average of $8.67. There was no valid way to tell the value of a ticket before the lottery drawing, but those who had chosen their tickets felt more positive about their chances of winning.

Studies show that people attach great significance to an unlikely event when it seems very important to them, whether the event is a hazard or a gain. For example, meltdown of a nuclear power plant is a highly unlikely event, but many people worry about it. Another example: Winning a major prize in a lottery is also highly unlikely, but such a prize seems so desirable that many people ignore how slight their chances are. In the case of lotteries and other games of chance, the overweighting of improbable occurrences might be called wishful thinking.

Overconfidence affects many decisions made by adolescents about hazards. According to Beatrix Hamburg, a child psychiatrist at Mount Sinai Hospital in New York City, "Adolescents tend to grossly over- or underestimate based on their immediate experience. When they say, 'Everyone's doing it—why shouldn't I?' they wildly overestimate the actual numbers. And by the same token, they wildly overestimate the safety of the dangerous things they do."

To an extent, risk taking is a normal part of the process during which a person changes from a dependent child to an independent adult. (This process is not confined to the teenage years. It may begin at age ten and extend into the mid-twenties.) Psychologists believe that trying new experiences and challenging rules is vital for personal growth during this period. But young people are usually poor judges of risk and sometimes act as though they were invulnerable to harm.

Teenagers, in particular, underestimate risks and feel "it won't happen to me." All too frequently, "it" does.

This reckless behavior takes a terrible toll: adolescents are the only age group in which the death rate has risen since 1960. For teenagers, life has grown genuinely more hazardous. Three-quarters of these deaths are caused by accidents, homicides, and suicides. Many can be traced to reckless behavior and faulty judgment in the use of drugs, alcohol, and automobiles.

Recognizing this rising death toll, the United States government and private foundations began in 1987 to plan research on the risky behavior of young people. This effort was welcomed by scientists, but some psychologists said that key elements of risk-taking adolescent behavior were already understood, just not recognized by many adults. Teenagers see the world far differently from the way most adults see it. They tend to be insecure about their values and judgments and to be susceptible to the influence of their peers.

For many adolescents, the greatest risk is not that of taking drugs or driving recklessly but that of social rejection. Beatrix Hamburg said, "Sometimes it is risk-avoidant to take a drink, smoke a joint, or have sex rather than be ridiculed, shunned, or deprecated by peers." Any program aimed at reducing risky behavior by young people must take these social realities into account.

Waiting for Earthquakes in California

Some of the mental strategies that people use to help make sense of an uncertain world were revealed in a study of attitudes of Californians about earthquakes. This research, based on detailed interviews at home and on the telephone with many hundreds of Los Angeles County residents, was conducted over three and a half years in the late 1970s. Public concern about earthquakes increased in 1976, as a result of media reports of earthquake predictions.

In their published report on this study, *Waiting for Disaster: Earthquake Watch in California,* researchers Ralph Turner, Joanne Nigg, and Denise Paz wrote, "The earthquake threat was acknowledged by nearly everyone in spite of failed forecasts, publicly aired disputes among experts, and silence on the part of political leaders. But it was seldom more than a fascinating sideshow to the main events of daily life."

The investigators found a great variation in the *quality* of awareness in the public—"the difference between knowing something and really knowing something." Thus, even those who were at greatest risk from dam collapses or runaway brush fires as a result of a quake were blithely unaware of these dangers. Although people overwhelmingly endorsed more government spending for earthquake safety, they treated it more like a luxury than a necessity. The people who were most aware and concerned were those who had suffered injury or loss in a previous earthquake or had a relative or close friend who had this experience. When asked about the hazards of living in southern California, few residents spontaneously mentioned earthquakes.

These people were not denying the threat of this natural disaster. Few doubted that a damaging earthquake would eventually occur. Many asked for more rather than less media attention to earthquakes. Most of those who heard conflicting information kept open minds. Rather than deny the threat, people tried to make it more manageable, in part by assuming that they would get some kind of warning before a great earthquake and that government officials were well prepared for it—wishful thinking at work.

People were well informed about what to do during a quake. Nearly all had learned that they should avoid elevators and windows and that they should seek shelter under strong interior doorways. On a personal and household level, this helped people feel that earthquakes were manageable. Jokes about earthquakes were common. The researchers wrote, "Acceptance of the earthquake threat as an appropriate subject for humor was a critical step in *normalizing* it—that is, treating it as something that could be acknowledged without substantially disrupting normal life routines."

People in California who had actually experienced loss from an earthquake were most worried about this hazard.

The film *Jaws* and its sequels made people highly conscious of shark attack on humans (in reality, a very low risk).

The "Availability" Factor

People clearly have a tendency to exaggerate some hazards and to minimize others. Psychologists call a key factor in these choices the "availability" factor.

Whether a hazard is "available" to a person depends partly on how memorable or imaginable the hazard is. If, for example, you recently saw a frightening film about a human-eating shark, the experience is easy to remember and imagine and, therefore, readily available to influence your perceptions about the risk of shark attack. The film *Jaws,* and its sequels, certainly made swimming *seem* more risky and reportedly kept some people out of the water at ocean beaches.

In 1986, a terrorist attack that killed United States citizens at the airport in Athens, Greece, prompted nearly 2 million Americans to cancel European travel plans for later that year. The "availability" of the terrorist attack in people's imaginations plainly had a marked effect on their perceptions of risk.

At Decision Research in Eugene, Oregon, psychologists Paul Slovic, Baruch Fischhoff, and colleagues investigated this type of reasoning by asking people to judge the frequency of various causes of death. They found that rare causes of death were overestimated and common causes were underestimated. Dramatic events that often claim numerous victims—tornadoes, floods, fires—were overestimated. Undramatic killers of one person at a time—asthma, diabetes, stroke—were underestimated. Most people judged that asthma and tornadoes each kill about 500 people a year. In fact, tornadoes kill about 100 and asthma about 3,000.

Slovic and his colleagues warned that judgments based on "availability" can be major obstacles to educating people about risks or to having open discussions about such risks. In 1979 they wrote, "Consider an engineer demonstrating the safety of subterranean nuclear waste disposal" by pointing out the improbability of various problems occurring. "Rather than reassuring the audience, the presentation might lead individuals to feel that 'I didn't realize there were so many things that could go wrong.' "

Experts and Nonexperts

In the matter of nuclear waste storage and countless other controversial issues, there is a wide gap between the risk perceptions of experts and those of the general public. To understand why, in the late 1970s, Paul Slovic and his colleagues at Decision Research asked four different groups to make judgments about the risk of death from thirty different activities and technologies, ranging from nuclear power to bicycle riding. The groups were college students, members of the League of Women Voters, members of a club for business and professional people, and "experts"—fifteen people from across the United States who were actually involved professionally in risk assessment.

All four groups had similar opinions about some items on the list. All judged smoking, handguns, and motorcycles to be quite risky. In some cases, however, the three groups of nonexperts disagreed markedly with the experts. Most striking was the difference of opinion about nuclear power. The experts ranked it number twenty out of thirty as a hazard, judging it to be less dangerous than bicycling and railroads. The businessmen's group ranked it eighth. Students and members of the League of Women Voters ranked nuclear power number one in riskiness.

In further research the psychologists found the best available estimates of the annual deaths from most of the activities or technologies on the list (some had no known deaths or estimates). Then they compared these data with the rankings of risk made by the different groups. Not surprisingly, they found that the experts' judgments about risks were close to the ranking based on death statistics—so close, in fact, that it "seemed reasonable to conclude that they viewed the risk of an activity or technology as synonymous with its annual fatalities."

The researchers wondered why nonexperts appeared to mis-

How Risky Is It?

Activity or technology	League of Women Voters	College students	Business club members	Experts
Nuclear power	1	1	8	20
Motor vehicles	2	5	3	1
Handguns	3	2	1	4
Smoking	4	3	4	2
Motorcycles	5	6	2	6
Alcoholic beverages	6	7	5	3
General (private) aviation	7	15	11	12
Police work	8	8	7	17
Pesticides	9	4	15	8
Surgery	10	11	9	5
Fire fighting	11	10	6	18
Large construction	12	14	13	13
Hunting	13	18	10	23
Spray cans	14	13	23	26
Mountain climbing	15	22	12	29
Bicycles	16	24	14	15
Commercial aviation	17	16	18	16
Electric power (non-nuclear)	18	19	19	9
Swimming	19	30	17	10
Contraceptives	20	9	22	11
Skiing	21	25	16	30
X rays	22	17	24	7
High school and college football	23	26	21	27
Railroads	24	23	20	19
Food preservatives	25	12	28	14
Food coloring	26	20	30	21
Power mowers	27	28	25	28
Prescription antibiotics	28	21	26	24
Home appliances	29	27	27	22
Vaccinations	30	29	29	25

Members of our groups were asked to rank thirty activities or technologies, with number 1 being most risky, number 30 least risky. Experts on risk assessment seemed to base their judgment on actual death statistics, non-experts on other characteristics of the hazard.

judge the danger of certain activities or technologies. Were they just too poorly informed to make more accurate judgments? The researchers then asked the nonexperts to estimate the average annual deaths caused by different items on the list. Surprisingly, their death estimates sometimes varied considerably from their ranking of a technology's danger. This was especially striking in the case of nuclear power. Most nonexperts had rated it first among risks but put it last in their estimates of actual deaths.

It seemed that ordinary people brought factors other than annual fatalities into their concept of risk. They were concerned with more subtle effects than deaths in an average year. For example, questioning revealed that the disaster potential of nuclear power loomed large in the feelings of people.

Exploring this further, the researchers devised a questionnaire about ninety different activities or technologies. People were asked to judge some key qualities of such activities or technologies as bicycling, smoking, skiing, X rays, police work, and nuclear power.

Some of these qualities included the following: Do people face this hazard voluntarily or involuntarily? Is death immediate or likely to occur at some later time? If you are exposed to the hazard, to what extent can you, by personal skill or diligence, avoid death? Is this hazard new and novel or old and familiar? Is this a hazard that kills people one at a time (chronic) or one that kills large numbers of people at once (catastrophic)? Is this a hazard that people have learned to live with and can think about reasonably calmly, or is it one that people have great dread of?

The Dread Factor

These questions took people into broader, much more complex considerations than annual death statistics. Nuclear power had the dubious distinction of scoring at or near the extreme of all negative characteristics. People saw its hazards as involuntary, delayed, unknown, uncontrollable, unfamiliar, potentially cata-

How People Rate the Qualities of Hazards

Some hazards are familiar and have qualities, listed at the bottom and left side of chart, that make them much more acceptable than hazards that are dreaded and unfamiliar, which have the characteristics listed at the top and right side of the chart.

strophic, dreaded, and severe. Paul Slovic combined several of these characteristics into one that he calls the *dread factor*. Nuclear power, nuclear weapons, and terrorism score highest on the characteristics that make up this factor.

By contrast, people judged the hazards of X-ray radiation and non-nuclear electric power to be much lower. These technologies, they believed, presented risks that were much more voluntary, less catastrophic, less dreaded, and more familiar than nuclear power.

All of these studies showed dramatically that risk means different things to different people. Actual experts who assess hazards professionally define risk narrowly, usually in terms of annual deaths or some other *quantity*. The public cares less about numbers and more about the *quality* of risk.

"There's a kind of wisdom and foolishness on both sides," Slovic said. "Each side, expert and public, has something valid to contribute. Each side must respect the insight and intelligence of the other."

CHAPTER 2

Deciphering the Truth

We argue and will go on arguing about risk in two different languages: numbers and emotions, odds and anxieties.
— *Ellen Goodman, syndicated columnist*

Most people find out about hazardous situations from the news media, but television, newspapers, and other media sometimes contribute to our confusion, exaggerating some risks, ignoring others. At times it seems there is a "carcinogen of the month"—a newly discovered cancer-causing substance in the food we eat or the air we breathe. (In the late 1970s one scientist kept a tally and found that forty to fifty hazards received national media attention each year.)

Television newscasts in particular have been accused of "fear mongering," of "victim-oriented" journalism. In 1987, Maryland scientist Thomas Sheahen pointed out that emphasis on events or technologies that represent great unknowns or dread provides "a perfect menu for obtaining high television ratings. . . . [T]elevision coverage tends to emphasize both the unknown and dread factors, thus pushing perception of risk further up." Indeed, television does influence the availability factor of various hazards, making it easier for people to imagine the worst.

For many people, especially senior citizens, television is the major source of knowledge about current events; many people

Train wrecks, fires, homicides, and plane crashes are the kinds of hazard

have neither the desire nor the time to dig deeply for substantial information about possible hazards. Those who get most of their information from television are at the mercy of its often simplistic treatment of issues. (Many newspapers also fail to provide much substance.) Local news shows, in particular, offer daily examples of this distorted emphasis. Images of fires, floods, train wrecks, and other natural or humanmade disasters are favored. Whether this kind of reporting causes viewers to misperceive the risks of life is a thorny question, one so far without a clear answer. Research has shown, however, that frequent viewers of television newscasts see the world as a more dangerous place than those who watch rarely.

In the study of public attitudes about earthquakes in southern California, the investigators asked people questions to determine which sources of information about earthquakes they took most seriously. Books and magazines were believed to be much more credible than other sources. After them, newspapers and television were considered about equally believable. Radio had about half the credibility of newspapers and television. Other people,

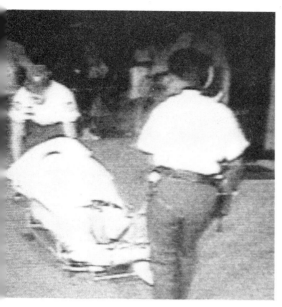

mphasized by television news reports.

as sources of information, had the least credibility of all, according to the study.

As the study went on, the researchers found that people relied less on television and more on newspapers for information. They wanted a better understanding of the earthquake threat and found much more detail in print media. Also, the newspapers of Los Angeles County had been skeptical from the start about a self-proclaimed geophysicist and his earthquake prediction, while television featured this pseudoscientist without investigating his claims.

Some observers blame television and other news media for what they consider a huge overreaction to the risks of life. In 1983, physicist Bernard Cohen, a longtime advocate of nuclear power, wrote, "Journalists have grossly misinformed the American public about the dangers of radiation and of nuclear power with their highly unbalanced treatments and their incorrect or misleading interpretations of scientific information."

Science writer William F. Allman has observed, "The media are more chroniclers of the extraordinary than a bank of information."

This was substantiated by a 1979 study of how two newspapers—one in Oregon, the other in Massachusetts—reported various causes of death. The study was conducted by psychologists Paul Slovic and Barbara Combs of Decision Research. They discovered that the news stories seldom reflected the actual frequency of death in the population. Diseases take a thousand times more lives than homicides, but the newspapers carried three times as many articles about murder. Such diseases as cancer and heart disease take about sixteen times the number of lives as accidents, yet the newspapers emphasized accidental deaths by a margin of six to one.

Slovic wrote, "The fact that subtle differences in how risks are presented can have big effects on how they are perceived suggests that people who present risks to the public have considerable ability to manipulate perceptions."

There is no evidence, however, that news media deliberately distort reality about hazards. Network executives, newspaper editors, and others who decide what is news are not risk-assessment experts. Like most people, they tend to focus on the qualities of events and technologies, not just on known or estimated deaths. Like other nonexperts, they often exaggerate dangers. Also, what critics call *victim-oriented* journalism may be the expression of a responsibility felt by people who work in news media to alert the public to hazards (called *duty to warn* by psychologists).

"Lies, Damned Lies, and Statistics"

Questions about distortions can also be aimed at risk assessments made by experts. For example, a controversial comparison of risks was published in 1979 by Richard Wilson of the Department of Physics and Environmental Policy at Harvard University. Using the best available data or estimates of various hazards, he calculated how much exposure to the hazard would increase a person's chance of dying in any year by one in a million. A table of these comparisons is shown on the next page.

Risks that Increase Chance of Death by One in a Million

Smoking 1.4 cigarettes	Cancer, heart disease
Drinking ½ liter of wine	Cirrhosis of the liver
Spending 1 hour in a coal mine	Black lung disease
Spending 3 hours in a coal mine	Accident
Living 2 days in New York or Boston	Air pollution
Traveling 6 minutes by canoe	Accident
Traveling 10 miles by bicycle	Accident
Traveling 30 miles by car	Accident
Flying 1,000 miles by jet	Accident
Flying 6,000 miles by jet	Cancer caused by cosmic radiation
Living 2 months in Denver on vacation from New York	Cancer caused by cosmic radiation
Living 2 months in average stone or brick building	Cancer caused by natural radioactivity
One chest X ray taken in a good hospital	Cancer caused by radiation
Living 2 months with a cigarette smoker	Cancer, heart disease
Eating 40 tablespoons of peanut butter	Liver cancer caused by aflatoxin
Drinking Miami drinking water for 1 year	Cancer caused by chloroform
Drinking 30 12-oz. cans of diet soda	Cancer caused by saccharin
Living 5 years at site boundary of a typical nuclear power plant in the open	Cancer caused by radiation
Living 150 years within 20 miles of a nuclear power plant	Cancer caused by radiation
Eating 100 charcoal-broiled steaks	Cancer from benzopyrene

Richard Wilson, an advocate of nuclear power, used statistical estimates of harm from different activities (activity on left, hazard on right) to devise a table that stressed the low risk from safely operated nuclear reactors.

		Days lost
Days Off	Being an unmarried male	3,500
Your Life	Smoking cigarettes and being male	2,250
	Heart disease	2,100
	Being an unmarried female	1,600
	Being 30 percent overweight	1,300
	Being a coal miner	1,100
	Cancer	980
	Being 20 percent overweight	900
	Having less than an eighth-grade education	850
	Smoking cigarettes and being female	800
	Being poor	700
	Stroke	520
	Smoking cigars	330
	Having a dangerous job	300
	Smoking a pipe	220
	Increasing your daily food intake 100 calories	210
	Driving a motor vehicle	207
	Pneumonia, influenza	141
	Alcohol	130
	Accidents in the home	95
	Diabetes	95
	Being murdered	90
	Misusing legal drugs	90
	Having an average-risk job	74
	Drowning	41
	Having a job that entails radiation exposure	40
	Falls	39
	Walking down the street	37
	Having a safer-than-average job	30
	Fires and burns	27
	Generation of energy	24
	Using illegal drugs	18
	Solid and liquid poisons	17
	Suffocation	13
	Firearm accidents	11
	Natural radiation	8
	Poisonous gases	7
	Medical X rays	6
	Coffee	6
	Oral contraceptives	5
	Riding a bicycle	5
	Drinking diet sodas	2
	Radiation from the nuclear industry	.02

Bernard Cohen's Life Expectancy Reduction scale estimated the loss of days from a person's life as a result of various hazards, diseases, and activities or conditions. Its narrow focus on statistics has little to do with the way ordinary people judge the hazards of life.

These calculations indicate, for example, that the risk of travel in a jet airliner is much less than the risk of travel by car, bike, or canoe. Most fascinating of all, however, are comparisons of familiar, everyday events (eating peanut butter) with activities or situations not experienced by most people (spending three hours in a coal mine or living near a nuclear power plant).

According to Wilson's calculations, eating forty tablespoons of peanut butter is as dangerous as living at the boundary of a nuclear power plant for five years. The health hazard from the power plant is cancer caused by low-level releases of radiation. From peanut butter it is liver cancer caused by aflatoxin, a substance produced by molds that sometimes grow on nuts and grains. (By 1987, the evidence showing aflatoxin to be a common human carcinogen was challenged; see further details in Chapter 6 on page 84.)

A similar analysis of various risks was prepared in 1979 by Bernard Cohen of the University of Pittsburgh. He used known and estimated death statistics to calculate how much time, in days, a person's life would be shortened by different hazards, activities, and diseases. (The table appears at left.) Some of the most dangerous risks were heart disease (an average loss of 2,100 days of life expectancy), being 30 percent overweight (loss of 1,300 days), and being a coal miner (loss of 1,100 days).

Comparing items and numbers on Cohen's Life Expectancy Reduction (LER) scale, as he called it, reveals that smoking a pipe (loss of 220 days) is somewhat safer than smoking cigars (loss of 330 days). It is also interesting to note that being poor and having less than an eighth-grade education reduces a person's life expectancy (by 700 and 850 days, respectively). At the very bottom of Cohen's LER scale is radiation from the nuclear industry—according to his calculations the safest of all technologies and activities listed.

The mathematics of Cohen and Wilson appeared to be accurate but reminded some observers of an old saying, usually attributed to Benjamin Disraeli—"There are three kinds of lies: lies, damned lies, and statistics." A narrow focus on numbers can mislead or confuse ordinary people, who, we have learned, judge risks in a broad, complex way. Many people know that commercial nuclear power plants in the United States have a good safety record, in terms of death from radiation—*so far.* But they also realize that a catastrophic accident could do such enormous harm that previous decades of safety statistics would become irrelevant. So, despite statistics, many people still consider nuclear power a greater risk than, say, flying in a jet airliner.

Can Public Fears Be Eased by Education?

Some business people and politicians have no patience for the public worry about hazards in the environment. They suggest that concerned citizens may lack fortitude, that there's something sissyish about this anxiety over modern life. They label it *techno-phobia:* fear of technology. And the cure for this "emotionalism," as they call it, is to educate people, in part by reducing the distortion of television and other news media.

In 1984 the United States Department of Energy (DOE) granted research funds to a psychiatrist who aimed to study public fears of nuclear power. According to a DOE statement, the study's basic premise was that "once people understand the principles governing the development of irrational fear, this fear will be substantially and permanently reduced."

Critics of nuclear power ridiculed the study, saying it was a thinly disguised attempt to suggest that opposition to nuclear power was a phobia. About the label *irrational* put on people's feelings about risks, Paul Slovic of Decision Research said, "It's not fair to call public perception of risk irrational, just because it differs from that of experts. There's no hard line between 'subjective' and 'objective' risk. Almost all risk assessment is based on judgments that may or may not be accurate."

As an example, Slovic noted that doctors once recommended

using X rays to irradiate tonsils. X rays were also used to treat acne, ringworm, and many other disorders and ailments. Not until the 1940s were the cancer-causing effects of X rays recognized. "Who really knows what the risks of nuclear energy are?" Slovic asks. "Because we don't absolutely know, we fear it. That's how people are, and policy makers must learn to live with the fact."

Proponents of nuclear power misunderstand human behavior when they believe they can simply educate people to feel comfortable with it. Beliefs change slowly and persist strongly in the face of contrary evidence. Once an initial belief is formed, a person tends to select new evidence that supports that belief. Contrary evidence may be discounted or dismissed. In the case of nuclear power and of other technologies that many feel are highly risky, only massive evidence of safety could begin to sway their feelings. Meanwhile, mishaps continue to occur that reinforce public skepticism.

Signal Events

Major mishaps can leave strong impressions. Some qualify as *signal events* that have far-reaching effects, like ripples spreading outward from the splash of a stone in water. The 1979 accident at the Three Mile Island (TMI) nuclear plant in Pennsylvania was such an event. It signaled overlooked problems that eventually cost utility customers and stockholders across the nation billions of dollars because of stricter safety regulations.

The TMI accident also sent a message to the general public. Even though no disaster occurred, the crisis at the plant seemed to show that experts had misjudged the safety of nuclear power. This strong signal probably also caused people to look more skeptically at other complex technologies.

Since 1979 a succession of disastrous technological signal events has occurred. They include the discovery of toxic waste contamination at the Love Canal site in New York State and the town

The 1979 accident at the Three Mile Island nuclear plant had far-reaching effects on the nuclear power industry.

of Times Beach, Missouri; the 1984 Bhopal, India, chemical plant disaster; the 1986 explosion of the space shuttle *Challenger;* and the 1986 nuclear plant accident at Chernobyl in the Soviet Union.

With the exception of the Bhopal tragedy, these events did not involve massive loss of life. In any given year an earthquake may kill more people. But earthquakes, train wrecks, and similar disasters are familiar and an accepted part of life for most people who hear about them. The signal events of recent years had much greater impact because they involved unfamiliar technologies and reminded people that it is sometimes risky to put one's life in the hands of experts.

We seem to dread most technologies that puncture our feelings of being in control. An essay in the February 18, 1985, issue of the *New Yorker* expressed the ominous signal sent by the Bhopal disaster: "What truly grips us in these accounts is not so much the numbers as the spectacle of suddenly vanishing competence, of men utterly routed by technology, of fail-safe systems failing with a logic as inexorable as it was once—indeed, right up until that very moment—unforeseeable."

In his 1986 book, *Normal Accidents: Living with High Risk Technologies,* Yale University sociologist Charles Perrow argued that such catastrophic signal events are inevitable because of the complexity of modern systems. "The sources of accidents are infinite, and even the best engineers can't anticipate all of the quirks." This may be unduly pessimistic, but it represents a feeling about complex technologies that is shared by many people. Further signal disasters will strengthen this feeling. This suggests that even greater effort must be made to avoid such notable accidents, not just to protect lives and property but to stop the erosion of trust and hope in new technological ventures.

Psychologists have learned a great deal about how people think about the hazards in their lives. This knowledge can be used to explain and forecast how people will respond to events and emerging technologies. Consider, for example, the known *qualities* of AIDS: it is a new disease, not well understood by science, almost always fatal. No wonder it is dreaded so.

The emerging technology of genetic engineering seems to have some of the same characteristics that make people wary of nuclear power. People give it a fairly high score as an unknown, dreaded risk. Release of a genetically engineered organism that proved to be harmful might be such a negative signal event that this technology might face the sort of opposition now experienced by the nuclear power industry.

When confronted with hazards, ordinary people consider vital factors that are usually disregarded by expert risk assessors. Industry leaders and government officials who ignore these public perceptions of risks do so at their own peril.

CHAPTER 3

Identifying Hazards, Measuring Risks

"There are no answers in toxicology, only opinions."
—Dexter S. Goldman, Laboratory Data
Integrity Section, Environmental
Protection Agency

It can be unnerving to keep a tally of all known hazards faced in a routine day. Furthermore, the general public is often unaware of health and safety threats that are known to scientists and to administrators of government agencies that are charged with protecting public health. For decades they have tried to identify hazards and estimate their risk. Even though these calculations are imperfect, they are the basis for government decisions about controlling hazards. For their own good, people ought to know more about how these matters of life and death are determined.

Some of our understanding of health risks comes from the raw data of deaths, diseases, and accidents. Such records are often the foundation of *epidemiological studies*—investigations of the relations between disease-causing agents and communities or populations. This method of investigation was first used in the mid-nineteenth century, in London, England, and the circumstances provide a clear example of how it works.

Cause of death was already being recorded in London when epidemics of cholera killed many people in 1849 and 1854. Bacteria and other microbes that cause infectious diseases were unknown then, and there were many notions about the cause of cholera. After cholera killed more than five hundred people in one neighborhood, a physician named John Snow drew a map pinpointing the location of each victim's home and discovered that the deaths centered around a popular public water pump. He guessed that the disease was caused by something in the water.

Snow soon learned of an opportunity in the south of London to test his suspicions about dangerous drinking water. The area was served by two water companies. When the companies had laid pipes and begun providing water about twenty years earlier, each had drawn its supply from the Thames River. But whereas one company continued to tap the heavily polluted Thames within London, the other took its water about ten miles upstream. As a result of this change, the stage was set for an epidemiological experiment, with water supply being the one variable between two groups of people.

John Snow wrote, "The experiment, too, was on the grandest scale. No fewer than 300,000 people of both sexes, of every age and occupation, and of every rank and station, from gentlefolks down to the very poor, were divided into two groups without their choice . . . one group being supplied with water containing the sewage of London, and, amongst it, whatever might have come from the cholera patients, the other group having water quite free from such impurity."

When cholera struck in 1854, Snow went to the home of each victim to learn where his or her water came from. There were nearly nine times as many cholera deaths in homes where people drank water from the polluted Thames. Snow's research led to changes in water supply and personal hygiene that reduced the death toll of cholera, decades before the bacterium that causes this sickness was discovered.

Death pumps the well water in this drawing made in 1886,
when contaminated water still caused much illness and death.
(Philadelphia Museum of Art: Purchased SmithKline Beckman
Corporation Fund.)

Cholera strikes quickly. Within a few days its victims are either dead or recovering. Given these conditions, an epidemiological investigation is easy; but today's chronic diseases, such as cancer and heart disease, are much more difficult to study. Chronic diseases may take decades to develop. To find their causes, epidemiologists often must look for clues in details from past decades of diet, smoking, drinking, and job patterns and years of many other factors that people may not recall very well.

In 1987, Lester Lave of Carnegie-Mellon University wrote that "epidemiological studies always have one or more of the following problems: too few subjects for confident conclusions, failure to control for important confounding factors, no data (or little data) on exposure, exposure levels many times greater than the standards being considered, inadequate diagnosis, subjects lost to follow-up, or subjects who are qualitatively different from the population to be protected."

Nevertheless, these studies have helped prove the dangers of many substances and activities, including nicotine and other compounds inhaled while smoking. No one can point to a particular cigarette as the cause of an individual cancerous lung, but epidemiological evidence clearly connects smoking and disease. In the 1950s, once doctors and coroners began recording whether patients and corpses were, or had been, smokers or nonsmokers, the data from millions of lives began to accumulate. Within a few years it became clear that cigarette smokers have a fifteen times greater risk of getting lung cancer than do nonsmokers. Expressed another way, tobacco causes about 30 percent of all cancer deaths in the United States. Smoking also causes other serious respiratory diseases and contributes to heart disease.

Epidemiological studies of atomic war survivors in Japan have given us much of our knowledge about harm caused by certain kinds of radiation. The lives of survivors who were near or downwind from the Chernobyl nuclear plant and who were exposed to radioactive fallout from the 1986 accident are also being closely observed by epidemiologists. Studies like these will continue to add to our understanding of diseases and other hazards of life. Their results are usually not as definitive as scientists would like, in part because some people or employers refuse to provide information. As one doctor lamented, "It is as if John Snow had been denied access to the names and addresses of the cholera victims for fear that the water companies might sue, or out of general concern to protect the privacy of cholera victims and their families."

Evidence from epidemiological studies clearly links smoking and disease, especially lung cancer.

Rats and Other Stand-ins for Humans

Early in this century, human volunteers were used to test the health effects of some commonly used food preservatives. Today such products as medicinal drugs, cosmetics, and food additives may still be tested on human subjects, but only after they have been tested on laboratory rats, mice, or other mammals.

Each year millions of rodents are used as surrogates for people. More than three hundred testing laboratories do most of this work; it's a billion dollar industry. Testing the effects of a single drug, food additive, pesticide ingredient, or other chemical usually requires six hundred mice or rats. Some, called controls, are not exposed to the chemical. The others may be split into two or three groups so that different dosages of the chemical are tested.

These animal *bioassays,* as the tests are called, usually last two years. Doing one correctly requires great care, effort, and expense—as much as a half million dollars. The rodents must be fed measured doses of a substance daily for two years. All of the rats are weighed at least twice a week. Every one that dies prematurely must be examined and samples of its body tissues and organs stored. At the end of the study, every surviving rat is killed. Up to a dozen tissue samples from different organs are taken from each animal and preserved. A typical bioassay yields more than 250,000 microscope slides that must be examined to compare the incidence of tumors or other abnormal growths in the control group with those that were exposed to the chemical.

Once the analysis is completed, certain questions must be answered. If a difference is found, is it statistically significant or a chance happening? Statistical tests can be used to help determine this, but with varying degrees of confidence. Can the findings in the rodent tests be applied to humans? Yes, but again there are difficulties that keep scientists from assuming that bioassay results are always applicable to people.

An adverse reaction in rats or mice does not prove that an

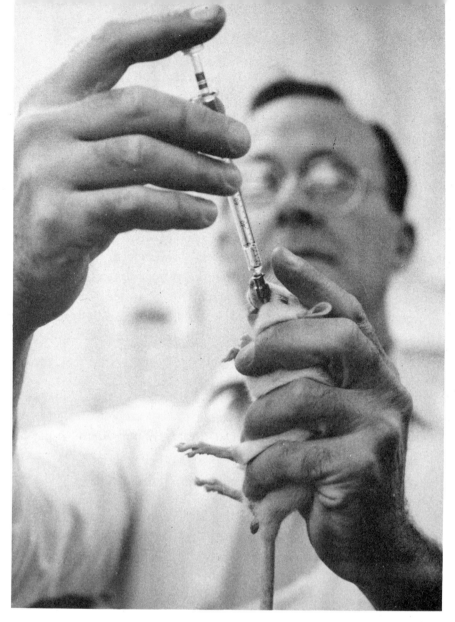

A rat is not an ideal stand-in for humans, but results of chemical tests on rats can often be applied to people.

adverse reaction will occur in humans. Also, a chemical that causes no apparent harm in rodents may still harm humans. No one kind of small mammal is an ideal model for humans. The drug thalidomide, for example, caused birth defects in rabbits, monkeys, and people, but not in rats. People and dogs get bladder cancer from benzidine (used in the manufacture of dyes), while rodents get liver cancer from the same chemical. A gas called bi-chlormethyl ether, used in laboratories, causes nasal tumors in rats but lung tumors in people. Another chemical causes cancer in the zymbal glands of rats. Humans do not have such glands, but this doesn't mean that we can assume that the chemical is harmless to people.

Extrapolating results with rodents to humans adds further complications. We live thirty-five times longer than mice and have two thousand times the number of cells. Mice and humans are much more alike, however, on the cellular and molecular level where cancer and many other illnesses take effect. Therefore, animal bioassays have proved to be valid predictors of several kinds of cancer in humans, of other adverse health effects, and of positive results with medicinal drugs.

Tests on small mammals will continue to be used to investigate new products and to help identify health hazards. But there are more than 60,000 chemicals in commercial use in the United States. These include 35,000 or more pesticides, 8,600 food additives, and 3,400 cosmetic ingredients. Many have not been tested thoroughly—or at all. According to the National Academy of Sciences, fewer than 10 percent of this country's agricultural chemicals and 5 percent of its food additives have been adequately tested. Drugs and pesticides are the most extensively tested substances, but health hazard tests are complete for just 10 percent of the pesticides and 38 percent of the drugs.

Each year, between 500 and 1,000 new synthetic chemicals come on the market and into our lives. Furthermore, there are many thousands of natural substances that have been tested very little or not at all; some of these may also cause cancer or other illnesses.

Cost alone keeps us from testing all of these substances with animal bioassays. Fortunately, new kinds of tests that use living cells, not whole animals, have been developed. Some can be completed in a few days and cost only a few hundred dollars.

The best known is called the Ames test, after biochemist Bruce Ames. He and his colleagues developed this short-term test over a twelve-year span at the University of California at Berkeley.

In the Ames test, some *Salmonella* bacteria and a food supply for them are exposed to a sample of the chemical to be tested. Other *Salmonella,* the experiment's controls, are not exposed. All of the bacteria are kept separate and covered for two days under ideal conditions for bacterial growth. Then the bacteria are checked to see whether growth occurred.

Ordinarily the strain of bacteria used *cannot* grow on the food provided. Growth occurs only after there is a change in the genetic material (a mutation) of some bacteria. Each mutated bacterium multiplies, forming a visible colony. Normally, some mutations occur in all of the containers, among the control bacteria and among those exposed to the chemical sample.

However, if the container holding bacteria exposed to the chemical has many more *Salmonella* colonies than the controls, this means that the chemical caused the mutations. It is a *mutagen,* and substances that cause mutations are strongly suspected of causing cancers. About 90 percent of mutagens have also proved to be carcinogens when tested on laboratory mammals.

The Ames test has already detected some cancer-causing substances in products, causing their removal from the market. It has stimulated the development of perhaps a hundred other short-term tests, many of which are based on its concept but use yeast, protozoa, fruit flies, and other kinds of bacteria as experimental organisms. Some short-term tests use rat or hamster embryos to see whether substances are *teratogens*—substances capable of causing birth defects.

The science of detecting harmful substances, *toxicology,* is only a few decades old. "Compared to other biomedical sciences, this one is an infant," said David Rall, director of the National Toxicology Program of the United States. "We're still at a point where it's pretty easy to criticize test results. But we have a tool for making important decisions, and we are quickly developing techniques to make those decisions more exact."

Toxicologists are relying more and more on short-term tests, Rall said. However, he concluded:

> For the foreseeable future, animal testing will be the primary tool for predicting toxic effects. It's not perfect. It's much better than it used to be. It can get a lot better. We need to work as fast as we can. The potential for tremendous harm posed by so many chemicals in the environment is so vast, so important, so overwhelming. . . . I think it's important to point out that most chemicals are not toxic. But our experience with a number of chemicals that have caused distress shows we can't ignore this problem. We need to get a handle on exactly what is happening out there.

How Risky Is It?

Once a health hazard has been identified, scientists try to determine how harmful it is or can be. Is exposure to it a major or minor health risk? That depends partly on how many people are exposed and how much of the substance they might eat, drink, inhale, or otherwise take into their bodies. Within a body, how much of the substance is absorbed? This is no simple question, since the amount of an air pollutant absorbed can be affected by a person's location (indoors or out), activity (at work or at rest), and even how he or she tends to breathe (through nose or mouth).

Suppose the substance is a pesticide used on apples. To determine human exposure, answers must be found to questions like these: How much of the substance remains on the apple? How many apples will a person eat in a year? Will residues of the pesticide remain in applesauce, in apple juice, in apple pie? If so, how much of these foods will a person consume? How much of the pesticide is absorbed within a person's body? How harmful is that amount likely to be?

Determining human exposure to such chemicals as pesticides sprayed on apples is a difficult challenge.

Answers to these questions lead to an estimate of a substance's harmfulness, for example, that it represents a 1 in 10,000 risk of cancer. However, the numbers give an aura of certainty that does not exist. As one science writer put it, "What eventually emerges from the estimates and calculations is nothing more than mathematics masquerading as science."

Scientists who assess risk evaluate chemicals one at a time. They may sometimes underestimate the danger, since people are not exposed to chemicals one at a time. Several harmful substances may be eaten, drunk, or inhaled in a short span of time. They may interact. Some chemicals are known to stimulate others to be carcinogens. Others stifle carcinogens. Some people are also more susceptible to certain diseases than others. Generally, scientists who calculate risk try to allow for these factors and overstate the risk of harm to allow for uncertainties.

Cancers may take decades to develop in people, so risk assessments about carcinogens are especially uncertain. Vernon Houk, an official of the federal Centers of Disease Control, has said that the difference between risk assessment and a five-year weather forecast is that with the forecast, if you wait five years you find out whether you were right.

Expressing the Probability of Risk

Most expressions of risk include information about the likelihood or probability of harm and its severity. It can even be expressed as a formula: *Risk = probability × severity*. For example: The risk of death in an automobile accident in the United States is about 1 in 4,000. (Probability is 1 in 4,000; the severity is death.) This figure changes somewhat with time and circumstances. It is based on fatalities as a fraction of the total population, which continues to grow and to age, with proportionally fewer young drivers. Also, high gasoline prices can reduce travel, and less travel means fewer accidents and injuries.

Data on auto accidents and other straightforward causes of injuries and deaths are easily expressed. Information on chronic hazards is less certain, and risks may be expressed less precisely. For example, one health expert estimated that "there is more than a fifty percent chance" that sulfate air pollution from a new coal-fired power plant would cause "thirty excess deaths a year." (A second expert estimated that there would be three hundred excess deaths a year.) Using "excess" or "extra" deaths is another way to express the estimated impact of a hazard on a population.

However, many people have trouble understanding the probability of risk. It seems to make little difference to them whether a given risk is one in a thousand or one in a million. Those who try to emphasize the minuteness of a risk by comparing it to one crouton in a five-ton salad may only succeed in making the risk more easily imaginable.

It is therefore important for risks to be expressed in ways that make them more understandable to ordinary people. For example, consider this statistic: On the average, 7.58 percent of women in the United States get breast cancer. This can be interpreted to mean that one out of every thirteen women gets breast cancer, but this is true only of women in their eighties. The incidence rates of breast cancer change with age. At age forty, about one woman in a thousand develops breast cancer each year, and at age sixty-six the incidence is one in four hundred.

Whenever possible, it is helpful to express a risk as one harmful event occurring among so many people at risk: The chance of one's dying of homicide in the United States in a recent year was 1 in 9,615. Another risk, that of a person being hit by a meteorite in North America, has been calculated as one in 180 years. People can identify with that one person, and the use of that "one" in expressions of risk helps them comprehend the other number.

The grim toll of automobile accidents can also be made more or less meaningful by expressing probability in different ways. Drivers are not impressed when they learn that a person's chance of dying in an accident on any one trip is about one in 4 million. However, according to Paul Slovic of Decision Research, "We make about 50,000 automobile trips in a lifetime, and the probabilities add up to a risk that is not trivial." In a lifetime of driving, about one out of every 140 people dies in an accident. In a lifetime, one out of three drivers is injured seriously enough to be disabled for at least one day.

An Index of Human Hazard

In 1987, Bruce Ames and colleagues at the University of California published a ranking of risk for some possible cancer hazards. A hazard's degree of risk depended on the potency of the carcinogen (determined from rodent bioassays) and an estimate of the daily level of exposure to the carcinogen over a person's lifetime. Ames called it the HERP index; HERP stands for *Human*

Exposure dose/Rodent Potency dose. It appeared in the April 17, 1987, issue of *Science* magazine.

The list of carcinogens included some well-known pollutants as well as common foods and beverages that many people might consider harmless. It even included carcinogens that result from the act of cooking food. Research shows that the burnt and browned material from heating protein during cooking is highly mutagenic. By 1987, nine different mutagenic chemicals that are produced during cooking had been tested on rodents. All were found to be potent carcinogens. The HERP index also included some foods that contain carcinogens, including bacon, peanut butter, beer, brown mustard, raw mushrooms, and basil.

"Nature is not benign," Ames wrote. "It should be emphasized that no human diet can be entirely free of mutagens and carcin-

In a lifetime of driving, the risk of being injured or killed in an auto accident is quite high.

ogens and that the foods mentioned are only representative samples."

In particular, Ames expressed concern about natural pesticides:

These are natural "toxic chemicals" that have an enormous variety of chemical structures, appear to be present in all plants, and serve to protect plants against fungi, insects, and animal predators. . . . They commonly make up 5 to 10 percent of the plant's dry weight. There has been relatively little interest in the toxicology or carcinogenicity of these compounds until quite recently, although they are by far the main source of "toxic chemicals" ingested by humans. . . . We are ingesting in our diet at least 10,000 times more by weight of natural pesticides than of man-made pesticide residues.

Ames warned that the HERP index should not be used as a direct estimate of human risk because of uncertainties about our knowledge. Also, his object in publishing the HERP index was not "to worry people unduly about an occasional raw mushroom or beer." Rather, Ames wrote, he hoped the index would "put the possible hazard of man-made carcinogens in proper perspective. . . . We also are almost completely ignorant of the carcinogenic potential of the enormous background of natural chemicals in the world."

Bruce Ames believes that the risks of some synthetic chemicals in the environment have been exaggerated. He called for a balance between "chemophobia" and the "sensible management of industrial chemicals."

Scientists holding different views criticized the HERP index. One argued, for example, that humans have been eating cooked meat and the natural pesticides in food for more than a million years and may have developed resistance to the harmful substances found in them.

Another criticized the HERP index because of its reliance on data about human exposure to chemicals. Ellen Silbergeld, a scientist with the Environmental Defense Fund, said, "Estimates of human exposure are poor, just awful. Assessment of exposure remains the weakest aspect of evaluating risks."

Silbergeld also said the approach of Ames's HERP index confined the national debate about hazards to one end point—cancer risk. "I'm not certain that cancer is our most serious problem. Lead and other chemicals in the environment affect the human nervous and reproductive systems. Exposure to excess amounts of lead can impair a child's mental development and reduce for life his or her potential and ability to contribute. Maybe this is worse than death.

"This focus on cancer," she concluded, "is extremely dangerous, because it distracts us from other effects, other concerns."

Whatever the merits and failures of the HERP index, its publication shows that science is a very human enterprise. Scientists try to determine the facts, as best they can. But they also have personal perceptions that are sometimes revealed when they choose particular facts and figures with the goal of changing public notions about health hazards.

CHAPTER 4

How Safe Is
Safe Enough?

*Then comes the issue of risk acceptance, a most
difficult step—moving from the world of facts
to the world of values.*
—*Cyril Comar, Electric Power
Research Institute*

Everyone makes judgments about the degree of risk he or
she finds acceptable: "I'm a careful driver; I'll skip the seat belt
on this trip." Or, "This chain saw is rated highest in safety; I'm
nervous about using *any* chain saw, so I'd better buy the safest."

In the everyday world, people use their feelings and values
when they decide the acceptability of risks. While measuring risk
is a scientific activity, judging how much risk is acceptable is very
different. In the realm of laws and government regulatory agencies, judgment is a very political activity.

As early as 1813 the United States government enacted laws
to protect health and safety. Efforts were made to guard people
from unsafe and ineffective smallpox vaccine and to reduce some
risks of travel by use of a steamboat safety inspection program.
In 1906, after seven years of debate, Congress enacted the Pure
Food and Drug Act. Since then, countless laws and numerous

government agencies have been established to reduce the risks of life.

The heightened risk consciousness that began in the 1960s led to the creation of such agencies as the Consumer Product Safety Commission, the Environmental Protection Agency, and the Occupational Safety and Health Administration. During the 1970s the number of federal regulatory agencies nearly doubled.

Each of these agencies has a specific responsibility, as defined by Congress. Many volumes could be written about them and how their actions—or inactions—affect the health and safety of the public. This chapter describes some issues faced by certain agencies and how those agencies make and apply assessments of risks.

Every day, people make choices about the risks they take, and the degree of risk they find acceptable.

Finding Carcinogens Everywhere

Since 1958, food additives in the United States have been subject to the Delaney clause (named for Congressman James Delaney of New York). It was added to legislation that gave the Food and Drug Administration (FDA) the power to require food manufacturers to prove the safety of new additives to foods. The Delaney clause is actually three clauses, which cover food additives, color additives, and animal drugs. The Delaney clause prohibits use of *any amount* of a substance as a food additive when that substance has been found "by appropriate toxicological tests" to induce cancer in animals or humans.

Once it was introduced in Congress, passage of the Delaney clause was almost inevitable; any member of Congress who voted against it would have appeared to be voting to legalize the addition of known carcinogens to food. But this clause soon raised difficulties. In 1958, when the amendment took effect, 50 parts per million (ppm) was about the smallest amount of a contaminant that could be detected by chemists. A decade later, amounts in the low parts per billion range could be detected. Now levels as low as 10 parts per trillion (ppt) can be measured.

At the time the Delaney clause took effect, the FDA believed that it was possible to keep almost all carcinogens from the food supply. However, it became clear that this was impossible as tests for chemicals became more sensitive and detected small amounts of more carcinogens. To many observers the Delaney clause seemed outmoded because it did not take the insignificance of such relatively tiny risks into account. It has been a source of controversy since the early 1970s, when the low-calorie sweeteners cyclamate and saccharin were reviewed by the FDA.

In 1970, completed animal bioassay tests showed that cyclamate caused bladder cancers when fed in large amounts to rats. The FDA banned cyclamate, as the Delaney clause and other food safety laws required. This caused no great protest from consumers because a substitute, saccharin, was already on the market.

Beginning in 1972, however, evidence began to emerge that

saccharin was a mild carcinogen. The Canadian government banned its general use after a study showed that saccharin caused bladder cancer in rats. In 1977 the FDA announced its intention to halt the use of saccharin in the United States. This aroused a storm of protest from consumers, politicians, and business interests, especially the soft drink industry. To an unusual degree, it also led the FDA and the American people into the muddy waters of risk assessment.

The process of risk assessment in government was not new, but it was new to the general public. At a 1984 conference on "Risk Quantification and Regulatory Policy," Washington attorney Michael Taylor explained why this involvement of the public was inevitable.

> The regulatory process is, for better or worse, open and participatory. It involves not just the regulators and the regulated, but also consumers, legislators, the scientific community, and the media, all of whom are asking the same question: How great is the risk? And most of them are looking for simple answers. . . . When the public debate begins on a specific issue, the pressure to quantify the potential risk is virtually irresistible.

The FDA's explanation of why it judged saccharin to be a health threat did not satisfy many people. Its announcement mentioned, for example, that rats that developed bladder cancer had received the equivalent in saccharin of eight hundred cans of diet soda a day. This brought a flood of ridicule, even though heavy doses are routinely used in rodent bioassays and are an integral part of the extrapolations to humans that result from these tests.

Donald Kennedy was commissioner of the FDA during the peak of the saccharin controversy. Concerning the kind of animal test used to establish health risks, he wrote:

> It confronts public skepticism—indeed, one might say it invites public disbelief—because of two stretches of reasoning

that many members of the public find themselves unable to make. One is from rats to people. I urge any of you . . . to try and persuade the average citizen that it isn't all that far from him or her to a laboratory rat.

The second problem is that of the dose–response relationship. People simply cannot understand that in a large number of cases, multiplying the concentration of a chemical tenfold increases the sensitivity of a test tenfold. . . . That logic, though scientifically impeccable, is impossible to make politically convincing. So a scientific discipline that is intellectually quite respectable . . . confronts intractable public skepticism.

Congress allowed saccharin to continue on the market, with a warning label about its possible harmfulness. This moratorium on the FDA's ban has been extended several times.

The Food and Drug Administration required a warning label on products that contained saccharin.

Meanwhile, the agency found different ways to interpret the Delaney clause so that it did not have to ban the vast array of substances in which traces of carcinogens are found. It was not trying to interpret the clause out of existence, but rather was dealing with new scientific understanding. The initial concern that we faced rare but powerful carcinogens in our environment had changed to the indisputable fact that carcinogens are widely distributed and vary a great deal in their potency. Furthermore, some carcinogens are initiators that prime a cell for uncontrolled growth; others are promoters that stimulate such growth.

Although the Delaney clause has many detractors and efforts have been made in Congress to change it, this law also has its defenders. William Schultz, an attorney with the consumer group called Public Citizen, said in 1985: "No one is saying that we can eliminate all carcinogenic risks. Congress is saying, 'Let's eliminate as many as we can.' There are some carcinogens that are unavoidable, but we can keep out the color additives because they're intentionally added."

In regulating food and color additives, the FDA has interpreted the Delaney clause as applying to the "additive as a whole" and not to all of its chemical ingredients. Some additives seem harmless but have unavoidable contaminants that can cause cancer. According to the FDA, the fact that an additive contains a carcinogen does not make it a Delaney clause issue but rather a general food safety issue. The FDA can then determine at what level the contaminant would make the whole additive unsafe and set a safety standard for its manufacture.

The FDA's general safety clause requires that food be safe, and that has been further interpreted by Congress to mean "a reasonable certainty of no harm." Some people believe that the concept of "no harm" means that the FDA cannot ignore even a tiny risk. Others argue "no harm" is not the same as "no risk" and that the term *reasonable certainty* implies the acceptance of some risk.

A safe level, according to the FDA, is a lifetime risk of one cancer in a million people. In other words, it does not consider a substance to be a harmful carcinogen if it causes fewer than one cancer in 1 million people who are exposed to the substance throughout their lives.

Some consumer groups protest that this is not safe enough. Given the uncertainties in risk assessments, a probability of one cancer per million lifetimes might bring no cancers, because a rodent carcinogen might not cause cancer in humans. Or in some cases it might bring several cancers, because humans might be more sensitive to a certain chemical than are rodents. If a one-cancer-in-a-million-lifetimes risk assessment proved correct, however, in the United States this would produce 230 cancers over seventy years, or three to four additional cancers each year.

In 1987 a committee of the National Academy of Sciences published a report called *Regulating Pesticides in Food: The Delaney Paradox*. It argued that there is a crazy quilt of regulations governing pesticides, with different rules for raw and processed foods and different standards for old pesticides and newer compounds. It criticized the Delaney clause, arguing that this rule may actually keep the level of carcinogens in foods higher than it need be.

The Academy's report cited a case in which the Environmental Protection Agency denied use of a new fungicide that would have been used on grain hops because the compound's residues posed a risk of causing one cancer for every 100 million people exposed. According to strict interpretation of the Delaney clause, even this small threat of cancer must be barred. However, this new fungicide would have replaced an older one—still in use—that posed a much greater cancer risk estimated to be one in 10,000. (Pesticide regulations enable the EPA to bar new products much more easily than it can remove those already in use.)

The solution, according to the scientific committee, would be to establish a uniform "negligible risk" standard for suspected carcinogens that would apply to all pesticides and foods. Rather than aim for the "zero risk" of the Delaney clause, the goal would be a risk the Academy scientists judged to be negligible: one cancer caused in a million lifetimes of exposure. (This is the same safety standard adopted by the FDA and, in 1988, by the EPA.)

The FDA and other regulatory agencies use computer models to help extrapolate the results of animal tests to humans, to estimate human exposure to harmful chemicals, and to make other calculations to determine whether a substance is a significant risk. Although the agencies use different models, the differences in results are often small.

Regarding the role of risk assessment in regulatory agencies, in 1986, W. Gary Flamm of the FDA's Office of Toxicological Sciences described changes that had occurred during the preceding ten years. He said, "We have gone from a situation where the

Stored grains are treated with pesticides whose residues may be eaten by people—another hard-to-estimate risk.

majority of the scientific community opposed risk assessment on the grounds that it could not be done with adequate confidence that the public health is being protected to a situation where the debate is now focused, not on the question of whether it should be performed, but how and how the results should be applied."

How Risk Assessments Are Used

Risk-assessment guidelines provide some consistency. They do not give scientific certainty, of course, but do help agencies set priorities and design regulations. Risk assessments can reveal targets for regulation and distinguish serious health threats from trivial ones. They can also give regulators the information they need to decide how stringently to control sources of a pollutant or other harmful substance.

Risk assessments were the basis for actions the Environmental Protection Agency (EPA) took against the pesticide ethylene dibromide (EDB). This widely used pesticide helped control nematodes (roundworms) and fruit flies on citrus fruits, peanuts, soybeans, cotton, and other products. Outdoors it was sprayed on crops and injected into soils; it was used indoors on stored grains and milling machinery.

Between 1977 and 1983 the EPA found evidence that EDB was a potent carcinogen in rats and mice. It was detected in fruits and uncooked grains, and surveys found this carcinogen widely distributed in the national food supply. Further alarming news came in 1983, when studies of groundwater in agricultural areas revealed that EDB was contaminating sources of drinking water.

In October of 1983 the EPA suspended use of EDB in soils. Then the EPA began the process of ending its use as a grain and fruit fumigant (a smoke, gas, or spray used to destroy pests) as well. But the process dragged on, partly because the EPA was required to weigh the risks that might result from fumigants substituted for EDB and because of the economic cost of banning the pesticide. Environmentalists claimed that the EPA was mov-

ing slowly as a result of political pressure from the Reagan administration on behalf of growers and chemical manufacturers.

Several states, including Florida, suspended use of EDB. In the
absence of action by the federal government, states also began to
set safety standards for EDB residues in foods. This threatened
to create chaos in national food distribution. Finally, in February
of 1984 the EPA suspended virtually all uses of EDB.

Scientific risk assessments were used whenever the EPA took
action in this long, drawn-out process. Studies showed that EDB
posed the greatest threat to workers who used it, and to people
who drank EDB-contaminated well water. This led to the emer-
gency suspension of certain EDB uses. Later on, knowledge from
risk-assessment studies showed the EPA that it was not necessary
to discard foods that contained low levels of EDB. The agency
then informed consumers that they need not throw away foods
that might contain EDB residues.

In the opinion of some observers, the EPA's risk assessment
did not go far enough. Richard Wilson and his colleagues Edmund
Crouch and Lauren Zeise of Harvard University pointed out that
EDB was a fungicide and was an effective control of fungi that
grow on grains. Some fungi produce toxins.

This is a "risk-risk" situation, in which the reduction of one
health hazard may increase the risk from another. Wilson and his
colleagues wrote, "Is the risk greater from using EDB than it is
from not using it?" This depended largely on the fungicides that
growers used as substitutes for EDB. Even though it had been
clear since 1977 that EDB might have to be regulated, very little
research had been done on possible substitutes—to learn, for
example, whether other fungicides were better or worse than
EDB at reducing the amount of toxins in foods.

The line between risk assessment and risk management became
blurred in the EDB case. In 1983 the National Research Council
recommended that regulatory agencies keep a clear distinction
between the two activities—risk assessment to be kept as purely

scientific as possible; risk management to be inevitably influenced by economic, political, and other values.

In reality, very few risk assessments are totally free of the influence of human values. Business interests complain that nearly all risk assessments are too conservative and that many scientists and the regulatory agencies exaggerate dangers. The choice of the individuals at risk or their exposure to a possible hazard, for instance, can influence the outcome of a risk assessment.

At a hearing in Massachusetts, for example, a public health consultant presented his analysis of the potential risk of dam-inozide, a chemical applied to apples to control the time when they are ready for harvest. Rather than the general population, he focused on infants and children. They eat more applesauce

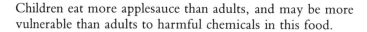

Children eat more applesauce than adults, and may be more vulnerable than adults to harmful chemicals in this food.

than do adults, and they eat more food relative to their body weight. Children, growing rapidly, may be more vulnerable to carcinogens. This scientist's assessment of the risk of daminozide was accurate enough, but his choice of children and their special sensitivity was a value judgment. Another scientist at the hearing also presented an assessment, one based on the general population, not its most vulnerable individuals. Each scientist had made a value judgment in his "objective" assessment.

The more uncertain the facts, the more likely that a risk assessment will be shaped to some extent by a scientist's or an institution's values. At scientific conferences and in professional journals there are increasing calls for risk assessors to reveal their assumptions clearly. Risk assessors are also urged to be more candid about the uncertainties. Policymakers, it has been said, only want "the number at the end of the study." Risk assessors can provide that number but should also convey how certain— or uncertain—it is.

Regulators, politicians, and the general public prefer certainty. However, this is seldom, if ever, possible. At a 1985 symposium on "Hazards: Technology and Fairness," held in Washington, D.C., Alvin Weinberg of the Institute for Energy Analysis suggested rather that:

> a far more honest and straightforward way of dealing with the intrinsic inability of science to predict the occurrence of rare events is to concede this limitation and not to ask of science or scientists more than they are capable of producing. Regulators, instead of asking science for answers to unanswerable questions, ought to be content with less far-reaching answers. . . . [T]hey should regulate on the basis of uncertainty.

CHAPTER 5

Managing Hazards

*We are terribly good, then, at finding small
amounts of something we think may be
dangerous, but we are terribly bad at finding
whether it is in fact dangerous, and even worse
at estimating how dangerous it might be. This is a
prescription for political difficulty.*
　　　　　　—*Donald Kennedy*
　　　　　　　Commissioner, 1977–1979
　　　　　　　Food and Drug Administration

The purpose of cost-benefit economic analysis is to assess in a systematic way the economic effects of government decisions. It has been applied to routes and rates for airplanes; to such safety aids as child-resistant bottle caps, auto seat belts, and air bags; and to the hazards of asbestos, cotton dust, and noise to workers.

Congress has specified that cost-benefit analysis must be applied to regulations that are proposed under certain laws, including those enacted to regulate pesticides, toxic wastes, and hazards to workers. On the other hand, the Clean Air Act specifically *forbids* regulators from weighing the costs of reducing pollutants against the benefits of reducing them. It was exempt from Executive Order Number 12291, issued by President Ronald Reagan in early

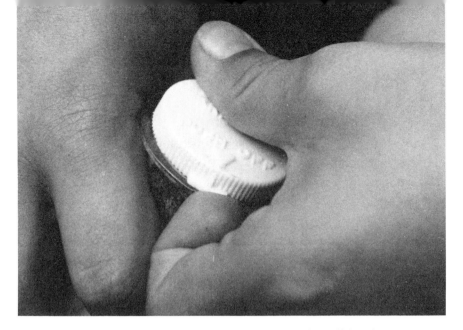

Regulations requiring child-resistant caps for pill bottles
survived cost-benefit analysis and have saved many lives.

1981, which declared that regulatory action could be taken only
if "the potential benefits to society from the regulation outweigh
the potential costs to society."

Cost-benefit analysis has been criticized from its very begin-
nings with the Army Corps of Engineers, which, since the 1930s,
has analyzed the costs and benefits of the dams and other water
control structures it proposes. Opponents of corps projects have
shown that its analyses of projects exaggerated benefits, underestimated costs, and ignored environmental impacts. However,
government agencies like the Army Corps of Engineers and private businesses remain staunch advocates of cost-benefit analysis.

Paul Portney, senior fellow at Resources for the Future, a research organization in Washington, D.C., also supported it. In
1981 he said, "To me, benefit-cost analysis is common sense.
The idea is that we don't have the resources to do everything.
So we have to choose carefully." He contended that cost-benefit
analysis does not always lead to less regulation; it can lead to
stricter controls on some health or safety hazards.

Opponents of this kind of analysis disagreed. They said that it
requires assigning dollar values to things that are essentially not

quantifiable: human life and health, the beauty of a forest, the pleasure of catching a fish or swimming in unpolluted water, the clarity of the air at the Grand Canyon or another wild scenic area.

Cost-benefit analysis is "basically fraudulent," in the opinion of Richard Ayres, senior economist for the Natural Resources Defense Council. In 1981 he said:

> They are trying to put into numbers something that doesn't fit into numbers, like the value of clean air to our grand-children. Cost-benefit analysis discounts the future. It allows costs to flow to small groups and benefits to large groups and vice versa. It is concerned with efficiency but not with equity. It is deceivingly precise and ignores ethical and moral choices.

Another critic was Ida Hoos, a research sociologist at the University of California in Berkeley. In 1982 she said that the cost-benefit technique was "about as neutral as asking a fox into a henhouse to observe the color of the eggs. There is nothing magic or scientific about it. It is almost always a . . . justification of a position already taken."

Commonly the costs of a proposed regulation are based largely on data provided by the regulated industry, and they tend to be exaggerated. Some benefits, for example, are hard to quantify; others may be ignored. In 1982, Nicholas Ashford, a professor at the Massachusetts Institute of Technology, said that cost-benefit analysis "becomes a very shaky game when it is applied to decisions affecting health, safety, and the environment." One flaw, he noted, was that this analysis ignores the long-term benefits that result when an industry is regulated. For instance, he said, when government regulations ban or restrict the use of certain products, industries usually develop substitute products that are less dangerous. Such innovations cannot be anticipated and aren't usually part of cost-benefit analysis, yet they are often a benefit of government regulations.

Nevertheless, the flawed process continues to be applied. An analysis prepared by General Motors shows some of the dilemmas the process can pose for regulators. General Motors calculated that the United States had spent $700 million a year to reduce carbon monoxide emissions from vehicles to 15 grams per mile. This prolonged 30,000 lives an average of one year, at a cost of $23,000 for each life.

Meeting a standard of 3.4 grams of carbon monoxide per mile would cost an additional $100 million. This would prolong twenty lives by one year, at an estimated cost of $25 million for each life, according to economic calculations from the auto manufacturer. General Motors economists pointed out another way to spend $100 million—by installing special heart-attack care units in ambulances. This could prevent an estimated 24,000 premature deaths each year at an average cost of $200 for each year of life. The auto manufacturer considered this a wiser use of money than further reducing pollutants from vehicles.

These numbers were concocted to help a business escape from tougher regulation of pollutants from its products. Nevertheless, this case illustrates difficult questions: How much is a human life worth? At what price do regulators judge that steps to save a life are too expensive?

The Value of a Human Life

People dislike the idea of setting a price on human life, but they routinely do so, in a sense, when they decide how much life insurance to buy or decide to accept a more hazardous job in exchange for higher wages. Putting a price tag on human life is also practiced by insurance companies, courts, industries, and regulatory agencies. Everyone agrees that life is priceless, but there are sometimes practical reasons for putting a value on it.

One way to figure this value is to determine the market price of a human body's chemical components. These include 5 pounds of calcium, 9 ounces of potassium, 6 ounces of sulfur, 6 ounces of sodium, and about an ounce of magnesium. In 1985, according to one estimate, the value of the various chemicals was $8.37. Other researchers contend that this is much too low. The market value of a person's blood alone may be $1,200, and the 140 grams of cholesterol in an average 150-pound person has a wholesale value of more than $150. No one takes these estimates seriously, as the valuable substances can only be extracted in quantity from a dead person.

Pricing life is not an invention of modern times. Throughout history, many cultures have had rules for compensating surviving family members for the loss of a life. The Aztecs had an elaborate system. In ancient England the word *wergild* meant "man's price" and referred to the sum of money or goods paid to atone for murder. The price was highest for people of high social status.

In the mid-nineteenth century, courts in the United States did not allow compensation for a person's accidental death. One judge wrote in 1867: "Looking at human life in the light of the Christian religion as sacred, the idea of compensating its loss in money is revolting." An injured person could sue and collect damages, but the family of a dead person was allowed no compensation.

By the late nineteenth century, however, courts allowed compensation for "wrongful" death. The amount was directly tied to a person's economic value. No award was granted for such values as loss of companionship or the emotional suffering of surviving family members. This began to change in the mid-twentieth century. Today many courts in the United States allow compensation for emotional as well as economic loss when a person dies. This is shown dramatically in cases involving the deaths of children.

Courts in the late nineteenth century viewed children as workers, as many were. Juries were instructed to calculate the damages for the death of a child in this way: "the probable value of services of the deceased from the time of his death to the time he would have attained his majority (become independent), less the expense

Court decisions of the late nineteenth century put little
value on the life of any child who was not working.

of his maintenance during the same time."

As time passed, however, compulsory education and child labor
laws removed most children under fourteen from the work force.
In the view of the courts, because most children were econom-
ically unproductive, they were therefore worth very little. History
shows some shockingly low court awards—of one cent, six cents,
ten dollars—in child death cases of the late nineteenth century.
In 1895 a New York judge refused to accept a jury's award of
$50 compensation for the accidental death of an eight-year-old
boy. He was outraged that a child's life had been assigned the
"price of a poodle dog."

Attitudes and law have changed dramatically in this century. Courts now compensate parents for emotional loss in a child's death. In one case, $11.2 million was awarded to parents whose infant suffered brain damage in his crib. (The child lived.) Thus a child that has little worth as a worker may be highly valued in courts of law.

The life insurance industry and government regulatory agencies usually assess things differently. They calculate the value of a person as his or her lifelong earning power. Inflation causes the price to rise.

This "human capital" approach to judging the value of life has many critics. Under this approach, women are worth less than men, blacks less than whites, retired people less than workers, and low-paid workers less than high-paid workers. Furthermore, it leads to the economic conclusion that death is preferable to disability, since a disabled person may not only lose earnings but also may sustain long-term medical expenses. Injury and disease are the most frequent consequences of inadequate protection from safety and health hazards, yet cost-benefit calculations almost always focus on lives lost or lives saved.

Government agencies use cost-benefit analyses to decide, in effect, whether certain lives are worth saving. Commenting on this, archaeologist Robert Zeitlin of Brandeis University said:

> We cannot argue that in our society human life has gained in value or that we cherish life more than primitive people did. I think looking back at our society thousands of years from now, people will regard some of the things we do with absolute horror, the fact that we knowingly allow people to die from environmental hazards, for example.

Regulators, defending the use of cost-benefit analysis, say it helps them decide how to protect the most people for the least amount of money. W. Kip Viscusi, an economist at Duke University and author of *Risk by Choice,* said, "The alternative is to pull numbers out of the air. . . . We always have to get back to the fundamental trade-off between money and risk, because we don't have enough money to eliminate all risks."

Viscusi is an advocate of the "willingness to pay" approach to setting a price on life. He and other economists have combined statistics on occupational deaths and injuries with data on wages to arrive at estimates of the pay that workers are willing to accept for putting their lives at greater risk. This method aims to calculate from a person's behavior what price he or she puts on life.

Suppose, for example, a job has an estimated risk of one death among every 10,000 workers in a year. Suppose also that workers are willing to face that risk for $300 in additional pay each year. This is interpreted to mean that the workers value the life of one of their fellows at $300 times 10,000 workers, or $3 million. Calculations like this suggest that workers in such highly risky jobs as coal mining value life at about $600,000. Average blue-collar workers place a higher value of $3 million to $3.5 million on life, and most white-collar workers are said to value a life as high as $10 million.

Union officials criticize the whole statistical basis of the "willingness to pay" formula. They also challenge the notion that most workers are free to demand higher pay for riskier jobs. "This theory has no basis in the reality of the American work place," wrote Eric Frumm, director of the occupational safety and health department of the Amalgamated Clothing and Textile Workers Union. In 1985 he wrote, "The recent deaths of immigrant workers in Chicago by industrial cyanide poisoning—not to mention the epidemic of asbestos disease faced by hundreds of thousands of uninformed American factory and construction workers—exemplify the lack of 'free choice.' "

W. Kip Viscusi acknowledged that few people choose their job with much thought about its dangers, unless the hazards are especially noticeable. He also said that "willingness to pay" should not be the only consideration of government regulators. "I think it's debatable whether, if a worker himself places a low value on his life, society as a whole should do the same."

Hazards on the Job

Much of what we know about dangerous substances, including carcinogens, has been learned by epidemiological studies of workers. Every day workers in certain occupations are exposed to higher levels of hazardous substances than those that reach other citizens. These workers have been called "society's guinea pigs."

Farming is the most dangerous occupation. It has an annual fatality rate of 49 per 100,000 workers—over five times the na-

Although coal miners no longer work with pick and shovel, their occupation is still highly dangerous.

tional average of 9 deaths per 100,000 workers. Coal mining is the second riskiest occupation, with 38 deaths per 100,000 workers each year. Mining, construction, and heavy industry—these are the types of jobs people associate with danger. But many other work sites, including artists' studios and hospital operating rooms, can be dangerous. Nurses and doctors who inhale traces of anesthetic gases, for example, develop cancer, as well as liver and kidney diseases, about twice as frequently as other hospital workers.

Since 1971 the Occupational Safety and Health Administration (OSHA) has had the authority to set and enforce safety standards for workplaces. OSHA is not required to weigh the costs and benefits of its regulations. Rather, its rulings are supposed to be "reasonably necessary and appropriate"—words that can be interpreted in different ways by workers and employers.

Like other regulatory agencies, OSHA pursues its responsibilities vigorously only when there is strong public pressure or when given strong presidential support. During the administration of President Ronald Reagan, the establishment of new safety standards and numbers of safety inspections by OSHA fell sharply. As a result, the number of work-related injuries and illnesses increased.

In 1987, Congress began to consider a law that would give workers greater notice about the dangers of their jobs. It was strongly supported by labor unions and some employers, and it was strongly opposed by the National Association of Manufacturers and many businesses. The proposed law, called the High Risk Occupational Disease Notification and Prevention Act, would establish a panel of health experts who would decide when the government should warn workers of hazards. Unlike existing OSHA rules, this law would require notification of former employees, going as far back as thirty years, and would apply to all companies, not just manufacturers.

Opponents of this law claimed it would create an avalanche of lawsuits from workers. Many of these lawsuits, they contended, would be based solely on emotional "cancer phobia," not on any physical harm. Even if most such suits failed, businesses would face great new legal costs. Critics of the law maintained that OSHA was already giving workers ample warning of hazards.

Supporters of this legislation argued that it would not start many lawsuits. To meet this objection, however, sponsors of the proposed law changed it so that workers could not use the expert panel's notification as the basis for suing their employers. Workers could, of course, still introduce the scientific information used by the experts as evidence in lawsuits. This legislation, if adopted by Congress, would be the most significant protection of workers since the establishment of OSHA itself. In 1988 it passed in the House of Representatives but was not voted on in the Senate. Its supporters believed it would eventually become law.

Workers often hesitate to fight vigorously for safer workplaces, for fear of jeopardizing their jobs. In 1987, for example, some workers at a Delaware auto assembly plant of the Chrysler Corporation expressed their strongest concern for the company, not themselves, when OSHA fined Chrysler $1.5 million for 811 health and safety violations. Workers there had been exposed to dangerous levels of lead and arsenic. Several workers reported that they worried about these hazards but also worried about the plant closing—"you hate to see something bad happen to Chrysler." Four thousand jobs were at stake.

In Tacoma, Washington, some residents and workers also felt that they faced a simple choice—jobs or health. In 1983 the EPA insisted on tougher controls on arsenic emissions from Tacoma's Asarco copper smelter. Asarco employed 550 people, paid about $2.2 million in state and local taxes, and spent about $49 million annually for wages, benefits, fuels, and services. The copper industry was not thriving, and Asarco, Inc., was considering closing its Tacoma plant. It hinted that further pollution-control costs would force it to act.

Although a great economic benefit to Tacoma, the smelter annually poured more than a hundred tons of arsenic into the air. It posed a cancer hazard to both workers and nearby residents. Children living nearby had high levels of arsenic in their bodies. William Ruckelshaus, then administrator of the EPA, ordered the agency to conduct an unusual program of public education and involvement in Tacoma. The EPA held a series of public meetings, attempting to explain in detail the estimated cancer risks and steps needed to reduce them.

Subsequent opinion polls of residents revealed that the majority considered the smelter a health hazard. Of people in the 18- to 34-year-old age group, 53 percent favored stricter pollution controls, even if it meant the smelter would close. Among people over 55, however, support for tough controls on arsenic emissions fell sharply. This may have reflected the poor job market for older workers. Their worst fears were realized: Asarco closed its Tacoma copper smelter in 1985.

Informing the Public

The Tacoma experience taught the EPA that it had much to learn about informing people about risk assessment and risk management. William Ruckelshaus wrote in 1984, "We must search for ways of describing risk in terms that the average citizen can understand." Providing information to people is a widely used way of reducing hazards. Compared to other steps, it is a mild, indirect form of regulation and one that manufacturers resist less than others. A detailed history of how information about hazards has been provided to people is presented in the book *Read the Label: Reducing Risk by Providing Information,* by Susan Hadden of the Lyndon Johnson School of Public Affairs of the University of Texas. She reveals that little information about hazards was available to consumers early in the twentieth century. In 1927, some states were still unwilling to enact basic safety standards, so Congress passed the Federal Caustic Poison Act. It required point of run off on the soil. Do not spray patio surfaces. Keep children and pets off treated areas until spray dries. May also be applied to the same areas with a fog or mist applicator using 1 part concentrate to 4 parts of water. Best results are obtained by timing application to coincide with greatest mosquito activity in early morning or night. Do not apply more than 13 Fluid Ounces of concentrate (0.2 pounds of actual Methoxychlor per acre). Treat as large an area as possible Repeat as necessary.

SCREEN PAINTS — For Punkies (No-Seeums) Protection: Mix 1 part concentrate with 4 parts of water by volume and paint metal screens. Repeat as necessary.

CAUTION: HARMFUL IF SWALLOWED: Avoid prolonged breathing of mist or contact with skin. In case of contact, wash with soap and water. Keep out of reach of children. DO NOT contaminate feed or foodstuffs. DO NOT store or use near fire or open flame. DO NOT re-use container for any purpose. Do not use in a manner not described on this label.

This product is toxic to fish. Keep out of all bodies of water. This product is toxic to bees and should not be applied when bees are actively visiting the area. Do not apply or allow to drift to areas occupied by unprotected humans cr beneficial animals.

LIMITED WARRANTY:

Buyer assumes all risks of use, storage, or handling of this material not in strict accordance with directions given herewith.

Warning labels can help ensure safe use of products, if consumers can read and understand the information.

the word Poison on labels for twelve substances, plus information for treatment if these substances were accidentally swallowed.

Sometimes tragic events stimulated regulatory laws that gave consumers more information—or showed that information alone did not protect some consumers. After several people died from taking a drug that the Food and Drug Administration had little power to regulate, Congress in 1938 passed the Food, Drug, and Cosmetic Act. This empowered the FDA to ban substances— acknowledgment that knowing about a product alone was, by itself, sometimes not enough. Between 1966 and 1970 three separate laws were aimed at protecting children, including the Poison Prevention Packaging Act that called for child-resistant packaging. It had become clear that warning labels did not protect children who could not read.

Today all fifty states and seven federal agencies oversee the content of labels and other sources of information on a wide range of products. The information can range from a few words about the ingredients in a candy bar to a seventy-page booklet attached to a pesticide container. It was such a booklet that led Susan Hadden to investigate the effectiveness of label information. In 1986 she wrote, "I wondered how the south Texas agricultural workers, many of whom do not even speak English, could profit from such a complex label."

Manufacturers of pesticides and drugs are required to provide the most detailed, extensive information. In the case of prescription drugs, however, it is doctors who are given that information, in order to prevent harm from incorrect use. The FDA's goal was to have fully informed professionals communicating effectively with patients.

In the real world that goal is often missed. The information itself may be far from complete, particularly for long-term effects of a drug. Physicians get it from medical journals, advertisements, drug company sales people, or such books as the *Physicians' Desk Reference,* which prints the FDA-approved package insert from about 2,500 drugs, arranged by their manufacturers. Even when doctors have sound information available on a drug, several studies have shown that many patients do not receive the information. Doctors tend not to give adequate information about side effects; patients under stress tend not to understand it. Susan Hadden questioned whether the present system of providing information permits or encourages people to make good risk-benefit analyses.

In 1988, troubles with a prescription drug called Accutane demonstrated how FDA warnings can fail to protect patients. Accutane, first marketed in 1982, is highly valued by dermatologists for treatment for severe acne. Early in its development, however, animal studies showed that the drug was a powerful teratogen. The FDA required that this hazard of birth defects be listed in the information given to dermatologists and also on the product's label.

European nations put more stringent controls on the use of

Accutane, and their caution proved to be wise. In the United States the drug was prescribed for many women who did not have severe acne, and the warnings about birth defects proved inadequate. By 1988, scores and perhaps hundreds of deformed babies had been born to women who had used the drug while pregnant. The FDA belatedly took steps to tighten control on Accutane's use and to do a better job of warning patients. One measure was to include a photograph of a deformed baby with the drug's packaging.

Labels on foods and many other products have many short-comings. They are based on unrealistic assumptions about the behavior and knowledge of the average person. One study showed that people felt better about decisions made in the presence of a wealth of information, even when that information distracted them from making the best choice. Other research showed that consumers had high regard for products with "certification," even those from nonexistent testing companies. Most people also do not understand nutrition labels on food.

A small portion of the population in the United States and in other nations—between 10 and 20 percent—aggressively searches for information about products. These people are highly educated and well-off financially. They tend to be wary when buying and skeptical of advertising. In contrast, people with less education and lower income are most likely to assume that they are well informed, when in fact they are not. Their lack of education makes them especially vulnerable to the hazards that are stated or implied on product labels. In short, Susan Hadden concluded, "The benefits of information provision have accrued mainly to the well-educated and the well-to-do."

Risk Management Dilemmas

Government attempts to regulate hazards range from warning labels on products to the EPA's purchase of the dioxin-contaminated town of Times Beach, Missouri. Regulatory agencies vary greatly in their success at reducing the health and safety hazards of life. An agency's effectiveness depends partly on the quantity and difficulty of responsibilities assigned to it by Congress.

The EPA already had a heavy burden when the Toxic Substances Control Act took effect in 1977. The EPA was asked to screen the thousands of chemical substances already on the market as well as the hundreds of new compounds produced annually. Just keeping up with new chemicals would require the agency to pass judgment on the safety of four compounds each day. The job simply isn't being done.

In addition to its task of regulating toxic substances, the EPA was given responsibility for toxic waste cleanup and, in 1986, for setting standards for safe drinking water. It made slow progress. In late 1987 the EPA announced that budget problems forced it to drop a key program—testing for and measuring amounts of dangerous substances that accumulate in human body fat. This program, begun in 1967, had detected DDT and PCBs in humans and had been invaluable in assessing the risk of chemical hazards. Scientists protested the end of this crucial research. But the agency's work load had quadrupled while its budget, after adjustments for inflation, had not grown during the decade from 1977 to 1987.

For several years the most ineffective regulatory agency was the Consumer Product Safety Commission (CPSC). Starting work in 1973, it was hailed by consumer groups as a powerful force for creating a safer, healthier home environment. It had broad powers over a wide range of products, many of which had never been regulated. The CPSC oversees more than 10,000 products of some 2.5 million businesses; the products are involved in about 30,000 deaths and 20 million injuries each year.

More than three years passed, however, before the CPSC established its first safety standard. The agency did not get enough funds to operate effectively. It also proved to be highly vulnerable to interference from the White House and the cost-conscious Office of Management and Budget. The CPSC was also hampered by a failure of its staff to set and follow through on goals. It began with a goal of dealing with the most hazardous products, yet did the opposite during its early years.

In 1978, writing in the journal *Environment,* Clark University research librarian Jeanne Kasperson reported:

> The Commission estimates that a safety standard for power lawn mowers could save up to 88,000 annual injuries; for bathtubs and showers, 88,000; for public playground equipment, 46,000; for upholstered furniture (a flammability standard), 45,000. Instead, the agency chose to develop standards

The Consumer Product Safety Commission deals with such everyday hazards as toy parts that can cause suffocation.

for such products as matchbooks, fireworks, pacifiers, and swimming pool slides, each of which will likely forestall no more than 10,000 annual injuries.

The CPSC did a better job of setting priorities in the 1980s, although handicapped by an inadequate budget. Public interest in protection remained strong, but the agency suffered from the lack of a "safety constituency"—a core of concerned citizens who would lobby passionately for safer tools, appliances, and similar products. This lack was a direct result of how people perceive risk: Such dreaded technologies as nuclear power stir many people to political action, but familiar, everyday sources of injury and death do not. Unless this changes, the CPSC may well remain underfunded by Congress and will continue to fall far short of its potential for making everyday life less hazardous.

Choosing between Risks

A good many regulatory decisions involve choices between one risk and another—a risk-risk dilemma, mentioned in chapter 4. For example, the EPA estimates that 750,000 buildings in the United States contain asbestos. It was once *required* as a building material in many communities because of its resistance to heat and fire. Now asbestos dust and fibers are known to cause lung cancer and mesothelioma (cancer of the lining of the chest cavity) in workers in the asbestos industry. Fibers flaking off walls, ceilings, and other surfaces where asbestos was applied may also endanger people who work in buildings, including millions of students in 107,000 schools throughout the country.

The EPA requires that schools be inspected for the presence of asbestos, and may require the same of all public and commercial buildings. School districts face enormous costs if asbestos must be totally removed. Moreover, unless asbestos is removed with great care, dust and fibers may pose a health hazard to the workers as well as others. The asbestos must also be disposed of safely.

There have already been cases of illegal dumping of asbestos and of careless removal work that probably posed a greater danger to health than leaving the asbestos in place. Even when work is done well, school officials and regulators often face a difficult decision: Is it safer to seal the asbestos in place or to remove it?

Another risk-risk dilemma arises in the use of vaccines that are given to millions of children in order to protect them from such infectious diseases as measles, mumps, rubella, diphtheria, pertussis (whooping cough), and tetanus. The latter three diseases are usually prevented when children are given one inoculation, called DPT. When DPT is not used, some children die. In the 1930s, before the vaccine against whooping cough was used in the United States, as many as 7,000 children died of this disease each year. The vaccine fell into disuse in Japan and England during the 1970s, and the death rate for children increased.

Tragically, some children suffer from a reaction to the vaccine itself. According to an estimate of the American Medical Association, of 3.5 million children inoculated each year, 43 suffer permanent brain damage. The risk of this occurring is tiny, but, as the slogan of a concerned parents group put it: "When it happens to your child, the risks are one hundred percent."

Parents worried about giving DPT vaccine to their children but its use did not decline because most states require vaccination against several infectious diseases before children begin school. Lawsuits caused one vaccine manufacturer to reduce production. Efforts are being made to improve the quality of DPT vaccine, but, as one researcher warned, "You can never develop an entirely risk-free biological agent."

By far the great risk-management dilemma of our times is the world's stockpile of nuclear weapons. It is also seen as a risk-risk problem by some, since the reduction of weapons could increase the danger of war. No nuclear-armed nation dares to reduce its arsenal so low that it will be vulnerable to threats and demands by a more heavily armed country.

In 1987, the combined world arsenal of more than 50,000 war-heads provided the equivalent of nearly three tons of TNT for every person on earth. Like Californians who live with the threat of a major earthquake, most Americans try to "normalize" the danger of nuclear war. But fears lurk—of war started by a computer malfunction, by terrorists, or by the sort of human error that people have come to expect in the management of complex technologies.

The Soviet Union and the United States have enough weapons to wipe out each other's population several times. Their nuclear arsenals could be cut sharply and equally without increasing their vulnerability to attack. A small but significant step in that direction was taken in 1987, with the signing of the Intermediate Nuclear Force (INF) treaty. The United States and the Soviet Union agreed to dismantle and ban a whole category of nuclear weapons. Approximately two thousand warheads with a capacity to kill more than 300 million people were to be eliminated. Negotiations aimed at much greater cuts in nuclear arms continued.

Nuclear weapons pose a catastrophic hazard to humanity, but hope began to rise that people might yet reverse the arms race and reduce its danger.

CHAPTER 6

Reducing the
Hazards of Life

*Yossarian . . . had decided to live forever
or die in the attempt.*
                    —Joseph Heller, Catch-22

As a society and as individuals, people wrestle with the questions posed at the beginning of this book—how much should we worry about the hazards of life, and what should we do about them?

Most people want more vigorous efforts by government agencies to make appliances, drugs, and workplaces safer. They want more useful, clear information about the ingredients of foods and about medicinal drugs. Opinion polls show broad public support for these goals.

Each individual also has his or her own unique list of worrisome hazards. The following pages suggest steps people can take to deal with these hazards and to make their lives less risky.

Remember that life is comparatively quite safe. Without being a Pollyanna, it may help to keep in mind that we live in exceptionally safe times, in terms of the diseases and other hazards that plagued humanity for thousands of years. Worrying about cancer, for example, is a modern luxury, unavailable to billions of people in the past and still unavailable to many in poor nations because they will not live long enough. Many cancers take decades to develop; cancer and heart disease usually afflict older people.

The incidence of cancer in the world is increasing, mainly because of the aging of its population. This is true in the United States, where cancer cases may double (to 1.5 million a year) by the year 2030—simply as a result of the number of people who will survive to an age when cancers most often develop.

There is no cancer epidemic, nor is there likely to be. Although we now know that small amounts of carcinogens exist in numerous natural and humanmade substances, it is not true that "everything out there will give you cancer." Carcinogens vary widely in their potency, and many of the most potent ones have been identified and are being regulated.

Rates of some forms of cancer have declined, while others, including breast cancer in women, have increased slightly. Brain cancer and cancer of the bone marrow have also increased among the elderly. Cancers continue to develop in people in such occupations as mining, welding, and woodworking, and for those who work with asbestos or near coke oven emissions. The rate of lung cancer continues to rise, primarily from cigarette smoking. Unless you are a smoker, employed in a high-cancer-risk job, or are otherwise particularly vulnerable to cancer, there is no need to worry excessively. (Even if you are not especially vulnerable to cancer, there are steps described later in this chapter that may reduce the risk of this disease in your life.)

Be aware of how you perceive risks. Chapters 1 and 2 describe how ordinary citizens perceive risks and how experts often perceive these risks differently. Each way has its strengths and weaknesses. Even if knowledge about human risk perception does not change your behavior, it may help you identify voluntary and involuntary risks in your life, or realize that feelings of dread about some hazards may distract you from paying attention to more common and immediate hazards.

Keep in mind that people, with help from the news media, tend to overlook common causes of injury and death and emphasize less common ones. One researcher advised: "Don't swat at gnats when an elephant is charging you."

Some people insist on swatting at the gnats and ignoring the elephant. They may worry about outdoor air pollution while smoking cigarettes (inhaling two hundred known poisons, sixteen of which cause cancer). This is their choice, but they may benefit from being aware of the paradox.

Seek information. Sometimes the best available information about a health hazard holds uncertainties and may change. In 1987, for example, strong doubts were expressed in the journal *Science* about a common belief—that aflatoxins in peanut butter and other nut and grain products were a cause of liver cancer in humans. (Aflatoxins may only cause liver cancer after interacting with a chronic hepatitis infection.) Whether considering a change in diet or the purchase of a product, people need the most up-to-date, accurate information about health and safety matters. It is rarely found on television or radio newscasts or even in many newspapers, which offer little more than a headline service.

Books and such magazines as *Consumer Reports, Science, Science News,* and *American Health* are better sources for detailed, accurate information about health and safety hazards. Be wary of books about nutrition and diet; hardly a year passes without a best-seller based on inaccurate and even dangerous advice. Also seek information from local, state, or federal agencies, and from public interest groups. The names and addresses of such groups and of federal regulatory agencies are printed on pages 94–97; a reference librarian will help you find the addresses and telephone numbers of state and local agencies.

Assess your unique health risks. The life expectancy and the quality of life of each person depend in part on his or her genetic inheritance. People may inherit a tendency toward dental cavities or heart disease, for example. Only blacks suffer from sickle-cell anemia; many native North Americans have a tendency toward gallbladder disease. A person's age, home location, and job also bring different health and safety problems.

Some people are allergic to certain foods. Paying attention to information on labels is vital for them. Raw agricultural products aren't labeled, however, nor are all spices, colors, and flavorings listed on labels. The latter are often allergens. People with food allergies usually find safe products and rely on them; they must be alert to ingredient changes that occur with no warning.

Expect surprises. Once a year, sometimes several times a year, we are jolted by news that a widely used product is dangerous to health or safety, or that something goes awry in a technology which was judged to be virtually fail-safe by experts. Expect these events, then seek information to determine what danger they pose and what to do about it.

Change what you can. In 1986, EPA administrator Lee Thomas wrote, "We have . . . evidence that in many places the major sources of health risk are not industrial plants or even hazardous waste facilities. They come from things like radon, a natural radioactive product of certain types of rock, from the air in homes, from wood stoves, from the gas station and the dry cleaners down the street."

Major steps toward a less risky life can be made at home, school, or the workplace. So many deaths, injuries, and illnesses originate at home—in an unsafe power tool, a chemical cleaning agent, an unhealthy diet. In 1988 the National Academy of Sciences estimated that radioactivity from the gas radon causes 13,000 lung cancer deaths annually in the United States. Radon is a particular risk to smokers. It arises naturally from soils, rock, and well water and can reach high levels within homes, schools, and other buildings. According to the EPA, more than 8 million homes have dangerous radon levels. The EPA and also state and local environmental agencies provide information booklets and lists of reputable companies that sell radon testing kits. If dangerous

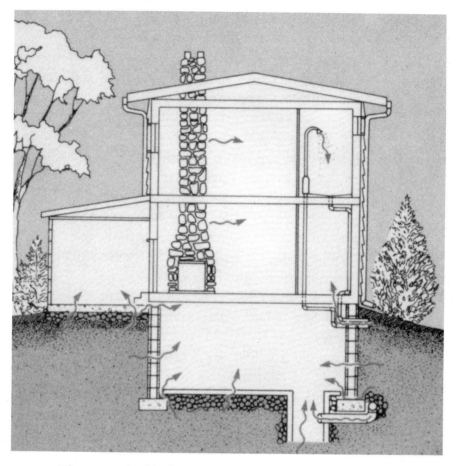

The arrows in this drawing of a house show common entry
points for radioactive radon.

levels are found, a number of steps can be taken to reduce the
hazard.

Also check the quality of the water you drink. Most county
health departments will test it, or recommend reputable water-
testing laboratories. Nearly one out of five public water systems
tested in the United States is contaminated to some degree by
chemicals. Drinking water is the most widespread source of lead.
The EPA estimated in 1987 that 42 million Americans drink water
tainted with unhealthy amounts of lead.

This metal is particularly harmful to infants and children, causing below-normal birth weight, height, and mental development,

among other effects. Most of the lead in water comes from water pipes and solder used in pipe joints. Since freshly applied solder dissolves easily, high lead levels are often found in the tap water of new homes. Consumers can protect themselves by letting water run awhile before taking a drink and by using only cold tap water for cooking and drinking (water from the hot water tank will have higher levels of lead).

Although scientists disagree about the harm posed by pesticide residues, there is no doubt that people are exposed to small amounts on a regular basis. The Food and Drug Administration tests for these residues; between 1982 and 1985 the FDA found pesticides in 48 percent of the most frequently consumed fresh fruits and vegetables—and the FDA did not even check for about half of the pesticides applied to food crops. Some pesticides are carcinogens; others cause birth defects or affect the nervous system or the body's defensive immune system.

Some scientists contend that these pesticide residues are harmless, but little is known about long-term, low-level exposure to pesticides in foods. Steps can be taken to reduce them in your diet. Washing removes some pesticides; others can be avoided only by removing peels, or outer leaves in the case of cabbage and lettuce. Peeling is especially important for produce that has been waxed, since waxes seal in pesticides and also have fungicides added to them. Sweet corn, bananas, oranges, and other produce with husks or skins that are discarded are much less contaminated than other fruits and vegetables. Finally, buy less imported produce. Tests have found that imported foods have pesticide residues about twice as frequently as those grown in the United States.

The dangers of pesticide residues, food additives, and the like are tiny compared to the harm caused by typical American diets. Perhaps the single most important step toward good health you can take is to adopt an anticancer, anti-heart disease diet.

The American Cancer Society's diet guidelines, aimed at re-

The safest fruits are those protected by a skin or husk that is discarded; washing also removes some pesticide residues.

ducing cancer, call for reducing fat and alcohol intake and eating more fiber—steps that also reduce the risk of heart disease. These are, in brief:

- Eat less fat, by eating more fish and other seafood, chicken with skin and fat removed, lean cuts of meat.
- Eat more high-fiber foods (including oat cereals, carrots, grapes, apples).
- Eat food rich in vitamins A and C (or which your body converts to vitamin A). These include oranges and other citrus, spinach, broccoli, carrots, cantaloupes, lettuce, and tomatoes.
- Eat foods that contain indoles, natural substances that block the activity of certain carcinogens (cabbage, broccoli, and cauliflower contain indoles).
- Drink alcohol only in moderation (no more than two drinks a day).

- Eat less salt-cured, smoked, or nitrite-treated foods such as bacon and hot dogs (read the product labels to discover how meats are processed).
- Eat less, exercise, stay trim.

Take political action. Without decades of public outrage and pressure on state and federal legislators there would be much less regulation of health hazards today. Membership in public interest lobbying organizations, as well as letters and telephone calls to legislators, can make a difference.

Some dangers touch not just our homes, not just the United States, but the entire globe. These include nuclear weapons and the threat of worldwide climatic change caused by human activities. There is also the matter of American manufacturers exporting to other nations pesticides and other products that were

An anti-cancer diet includes vegetables like these that contain natural cancer-blocking substances.

banned as hazardous here. Some of the public interest organizations listed on pages 96–97 work to reduce these global threats.

In political battles and debates about health and safety hazards, important words can begin to lose their meaning. Remember that there is a difference between a hazard and a risk (the latter includes an expression of the likelihood of harm occurring). Proponents of relaxed regulations on pollution, nuclear power, job safety, and the like prefer the word *risk* and emphasize that we must all accept some risks in life.

Langdon Winner protested against this emphasis in his book *The Whale and the Reactor: A Search for Limits in an Age of Technology:*

> A toxic waste disposal site placed in your neighborhood need not be defined as a risk; it might appropriately be defined as a problem of toxic waste. Air polluted by automobiles and industrial smokestacks need not be defined as a "risk"; it might still be called by the old-fashioned name: "pollution." New Englanders who find acid rain falling on them are under no obligation to begin analyzing the "risks of acid rain"; they might retain some Yankee stubbornness and confound the experts by talking about "that destructive acid rain" and what's to be done about it.

The political forces that want less government regulation of health and safety claim that some individuals and groups want a risk-free society. No environmentalist or other public interest group has ever sought this. People do not seek a zero-risk life. They do want a society in which most of the risks are undertaken voluntarily and with knowledge. They want the government to control serious hazards and to ensure that they have clear, sound information about others.

People accept the inevitability of risk. In a democracy they have the right to participate in the dialogue about how hazardous life should be.

Glossary

Animal bioassays—Experiments in which mice, rats, or other animals are exposed to drugs, food additives, pesticides, or other substances in order to determine the effect of the substances. (See also **Control**.)

Availability factor—A factor that affects a person's feelings about a hazard by the relative ease with which it comes to mind. For example, a hazard that has recently been in the news or which has harmed a friend or relative is readily available to a person's thoughts and feelings.

Bacteria—One-celled microorganisms. Most are beneficial, but bacteria are the cause of such human diseases as cholera, diphtheria, and typhoid fever.

Cancer—A disorder in which body cells grow wildly, producing colonies called neoplasms (tumors). Benign neoplasms are made up of cells similar to the surrounding tissues and are usually confined to one area. Malignant neoplasms are made up of cells unlike those nearby and tend to spread through the body. Cancer is the second leading cause of death in the United States.

Carcinogen—A substance or other factor (such as radioactivity or ultraviolet rays from sunlight) that causes cancer. However, some carcinogens are "promoters" that have an effect only if another "initiator" carcinogen has primed a cell for uncontrolled growth.

Chronic hazard—A source of danger that harms or kills people in an unspectacular way and, unlike an airliner crash that kills many people at once, does not receive much attention from news media.

Control—In an experiment, the standard of comparison needed to verify the results. For example, suppose some mice are fed a chemical in their food and many of them die. This proves nothing about the chemical and cannot even be called an experiment unless the results can be compared with the death rate of another, similar group of mice, the control group, which is kept under identical conditions except that they are not fed the chemical.

Cost-benefit analysis—A process of assessing the economic effects of taking an action by comparing its costs and benefits. This process is applied by certain government regulatory agencies when they consider banning a hazardous product. The process has flaws, especially the impossibility of putting a dollar value on many benefits.

Dread factor—A factor that stimulates strong negative feelings about a hazard. The dread factor has such characteristics as "involuntary, uncontrollable, catastrophic, having fatal consequences, and increasing in risk."

Epidemiology—The study of relations between disease-causing agents and communities or populations.

Genetic inheritance—The transmission of traits or characteristics from parents to offspring.

Hazard—A threat to people and what they value. (See also **Risk**.)

Human-capital approach—Judging the value of a person's life by his or her lifelong earning power.

Immunization—The process of becoming immune to a disease, usually accomplished by using a weakened form of the disease-causing agent to stimulate resistance to the disease.

Mutagen—A physical or chemical agent that increases the frequency of mutations in cells above the normal rate.

Mutation—A change in genetic material which may produce characteristics in offspring that are different from those of a parent.

Normalizing risks—A process of becoming somewhat comfortable with a hazard, acknowledging it without disrupting the normal routines of life. The ability to joke about a hazard is considered an important step in normalizing it.

Probability—The likelihood of an event; for example, the probability of a person's being hit by a meteorite in North America has been estimated as one in 180 years.

Radioactivity—Behavior of a substance in which nuclei of atoms undergo change and emit radiation in the form of alpha particles, beta particles, or gamma rays.

Risk—A measure of the likelihood of harm or loss.

Risk assessment—The process of studying and judging the actual harm posed by a hazard.

Risk management—The process.of taking action to reduce or eliminate a hazard.

Risk-risk situation—A situation in which action taken against one hazard creates or increases the risk of another hazard.

Signal event—As defined by Paul Slovic, an accident that "serves as a warning signal for society, providing new information about the probability that similar or even more destructive mishaps might occur within this type of activity." The accidents at the Three Mile Island and Chernobyl nuclear power plants were signal events.

Technology—The materials and machines that humans make and use.

Teratogen—A chemical or other factor that causes the development of a physical defect in a developing embryo.

Toxicology—The science of detecting harmful substances and studying their effects.

Willingness-to-pay approach—A method for putting a dollar value on a person's life, based on statistical estimates of pay increases that workers will accept for putting their lives at greater risk.

X rays—Invisible gamma rays, discovered in 1895, which pass through the body and leave a record of its structure on photographic film.

Government Agencies

Listed below are agencies of the United States government that have been given responsibility by Congress for matters of health and safety. Their roles range from inspecting meat (Food Safety and Inspection Service of the Department of Agriculture) to "protecting the health of the Nation against impure and unsafe food, drugs and cosmetics, and other potential hazards" (Food and Drug Administration). Each agency has an office of information that answers questions and provides free single copies of brochures and other publications. Information about health and safety hazards is also available from similar government agencies of states and many cities.

Office of Information and Public Affairs, Consumer Product Safety Commission, 5401 Westbard Avenue, Bethesda, MD 20207

Public Information Center, Environmental Protection Agency, 820 Quincy Street, N.W., Washington, DC 20011

Office of Consumer Affairs, Food and Drug Administration, 5600 Fishers Lane, Rockville, MD 20857. (The FDA also has consumer affairs offices in thirty-two cities.)

Office of Information, Food Safety and Inspection Service, Department of Agriculture, 14th Street and Independence Avenue, S.W., Washington, DC 20250

Office of Information and Consumer Affairs, Occupational Safety and Health Administration, Department of Labor, 3rd Street and Constitution Avenue, N.W., Washington, DC 20210. (OSHA also has ten regional offices in major cities.)

Office of Information, Public Health Service, 200 Independence Avenue, S.W., Washington, DC 20201. (The Public Health Service also has ten regional offices in major cities.)

Working for a More Healthful Environment

Numerous public interest groups seek to reduce the hazards of modern life by influencing legislators and by pushing government agencies into meeting their responsibilities. Many of these national groups are listed below; branches or similar organizations can be found in some states and large cities.

American Cancer Society, 1575 I Street, N.W., Washington, DC 20005

American Heart Association, 1110 Vermont Avenue, N.W., Washington, DC 20005

American Lung Association, 1101 Vermont Avenue, N.W., Washington, DC 20005

Center for Science in the Public Interest, 1501 16th Street, N.W., Washington, DC 20036

Citizens Clearinghouse for Hazardous Wastes, 2315 Wilson Blvd., Box 926, Arlington, VA 22216

Clean Water Action Project, 317 Pennsylvania Avenue, S.E., Washington, DC 20003

Environmental Action Foundation, 1525 New Hampshire Avenue, N.W., Washington, DC 20036

Environmental Defense Fund, 475 Park Avenue South, New York, NY 10016

National Clean Air Coalition, 801 Pennsylvania Avenue, S.E., Washington, DC 20003

Natural Resources Defense Council, 1350 New York Avenue, N.W., Washington, DC 20005

Public Citizen Health Research Group, 2000 P Street, N.W., Washington, DC 20036

United States Public Interest Research Group, 215 Pennsylvania Avenue, S.E., Washington, DC 20003

Worldwatch Institute, 1776 Massachusetts Avenue, N.W., Washington, DC 20036

Further Reading

Anonymous. "Radon Detectors: How to Find Out If Your House Has a Radon Problem" and "Ways to Make Your House Safer." *Consumer Reports,* July 1987, pp. 440–446.

Berger, Melvin. *Hazardous Substances: A Reference.* Hillside, New Jersey: Enslow Publishers, 1986.

Bodansky, David, et al., eds. *Indoor Radon and Its Hazards.* Seattle: University of Washington Press, 1987.

Brody, Jane. *Jane Brody's Nutrition Book: A Lifetime Guide to Good Eating for Better Health and Weight Control.* New York: Norton, 1981.

Brody, Jane. *The New York Times Guide to Personal Health.* New York: Times Books, 1982.

Connor, Sonja, and William Connor. *The New American Diet.* New York: Simon & Schuster, 1986.

Douglas, Mary, and Aaron Wildavsky. *Risk and Culture.* Berkeley, California: University of California Press, 1982.

Farley, Dixie. "Benefit vs. Risk: How the FDA Approves New Drugs." *FDA Consumer,* December 1987–January 1988, pp. 6–13.

Flamm, W. Gary. "Risk Assessment Policy in the United States." In *Risk and Reason,* 141–149. Alan R. Liss, Inc., 1986.

Fleming, Anne. *Teenage Drivers*. Washington, DC: Insurance Institute for Highway Safety, 1987.

Hadden, Susan. *Read the Label: Reducing Risks by Providing Information*. Boulder, Colorado: Westview Press, 1986.

Hoel, David, et al., eds. *Risk Quantitation and Regulatory Policy*. New York: Cold Spring Harbor Laboratory, 1985.

Imperato, Pascal, and Greg Mitchell. *Acceptable Risks*. New York: Viking Press, 1985.

Kasperson, Roger, and Thomas Bick. "The Consumer Product Safety Commission." In *Perilous Progress: Managing the Hazards of Technology,* edited by Robert Kates et al., 371–394. Boulder, Colorado: Westview Press, 1985.

Kates, Robert, et al., eds. *Perilous Progress: Managing the Hazards of Technology*. Boulder, Colorado: Westview Press, 1985.

Kerr, Richard. "Indoor Radon: The Deadliest Pollutant." *Science,* 29 April 1988, pp. 606–608.

Lafavore, Michael. *Radon: The Invisible Threat*. Emmaus, Pennsylvania: Rodale Press, 1987.

Lowrance, William. *Of Acceptable Risk: Science and the Determination of Safety*. Los Altos, California: William Kaufmann, 1976.

Marx, Jean. "Assessing the Risks of Microbial Release." *Science,* 18 September 1987, pp. 1413–1417.

Morone, Joseph, and Edward Woodhouse. *Averting Catastrophe: Strategies for Regulating Risky Technologies*. Berkeley, California: University of California Press, 1986.

Mott, Lawrie, and Karen Snyder. *Pesticide Alert: A Guide to Pesticides in Fruits and Vegetables*. San Francisco: Sierra Club Books, 1988.

National Academy of Engineering. *Hazards: Technology and Fairness*. Washington, D.C.: National Academy Press, 1986.

Nelkin, Dorothy, and M. Brown. *Workers at Risk: Voices From the Workplace*. Chicago: University of Chicago Press, 1984.

Nero, Anthony, Jr. "Controlling Indoor Air Pollution." *Scientific American,* May 1988, pp. 42–48.

Rosner, David, ed. *Dying for Work: Workers' Safety and Health in Twentieth-Century America.* Bloomington: Indiana University Press, 1987.

Turner, R. H., et al. *Waiting for Disaster: Earthquake Watch in California.* Berkeley, California: University of California Press, 1986.

Urquhart, John, and Klaus Heilmann. *Risk Watch: The Odds of Life.* New York: Facts on File, 1984.

Viscusi, W. Kip. *Risk by Choice: Regulating Health and Safety in the Workplace.* Cambridge, Massachusetts: Harvard University Press, 1983.

Weisskopf, Michael. "Lead Astray: The Poisoning of America." *Discover,* December 1987, pp. 68–75.

Zelizer, Viviana. *Pricing the Priceless Child: The Changing Social Value of Children.* New York: Basic Books, 1985.

Index